The Signal Between Us:
A Father/Daughter Discovery Story

A Novel

by

Ashley Rovira

Dedicated to the fathers and daughters of course—to the imperfect ones, especially. To all who keep reaching through the static.

Content Note on Mental Health

This is a work of fiction. The story includes references to mental health challenges, panic attacks, therapy, and recovery. These depictions are part of the characters' journeys and are not intended as medical advice.

If you or someone you know is struggling with anxiety, depression, or other mental health concerns, please reach out to a qualified health professional. Everyone's situation is different, and only a licensed practitioner can provide appropriate support and treatment.

If you are in the United States and are in crisis, you can dial or text 988 to connect with the Suicide & Crisis Lifeline, available 24/7. For readers outside the U.S., please seek local hotlines or emergency services in your area.

You are not alone. Help is out there.

Content Note on Substance Use

This book contains references to alcohol use, substance abuse, and related struggles. These depictions are fictional and are not intended as guidance, endorsement, or instruction.

If you or someone you know is struggling with substance use, please seek support from a qualified professional. In the U.S., you can call or text SAMHSA's National Helpline at 1-800-662-4357, a free, confidential, 24/7 resource for individuals and families. If you are outside the U.S., please consult local health resources in your area.

"Memory takes a lot of poetic license.

It omits some details; others are exaggerated,

according to the emotional value of the articles it touches,

for memory is seated predominantly in the heart.

...The past beats inside me like a second heart."

— Tennessee Williams, The Glass Menagerie

Prologue – Names, And I Knew

The signing for my latest book, *No Friend But the Night*, had ended hours ago, but the buzz clung to the room like perfume. I stood near the wide front window, watching the Bronxville street blur with the glare of the spring sun. Her name still echoed—Zoe MacKenzie, Carly's daughter, introducing herself with a wry smirk as Bridget's goddaughter. Bridget Nelson Cooper. She had said the name of my college sweetheart, her godmother, while standing before me, nervous and brave, dropping the names like anchors meant to steady her. And then she was gone, swept back into the crowd.

I exhaled, the fatigue of questions and signatures pulling me down. Outside, the taxi door was open, waiting. I paused, glanced up—and froze. There she was across the street. Her eyes locked with mine. The arc of time bent. The cosmos came to a screeching halt. A horn blasted. The driver barked at me to get in. The spell shattered. She was lost again to the moving crowd. I stepped into the cab, but my chest burned with certainty: I knew.

***

The car turns off the main road and onto a narrow drive lined with old elms. Roosevelt College sits like a jewel box at the top of the hill—red brick buildings with white trim, steep slate roofs, and the kind of lawns that look airbrushed. A small crowd of students and faculty are gathered at the top of the quad. It always surprises me how small and intimate these liberal arts colleges feel. Roosevelt is a regular stop for me on book tours, my publisher being a proponent of chasing the university audience. My publicist always picks Roosevelt among a crop of other New England schools, especially ones set in quaint towns where there are thriving local bookstores, public libraries, and plenty of suburban readers. That way we get the students, the housewives, the commuters, all in one stroke. By comparison to many of the colleges I visit, Eleanor Roosevelt College is tiny, with two main academic buildings, an athletic center, three dormitories, cafeteria, and the showpiece, sitting atop the hill, "The Castle", where the driver delivers me now.

The driver eases the taxi to a stop. A young man in a tweed blazer opens my door with a smile. "Mr. Griffin, welcome to Roosevelt. We're honored to have you here again."

I step out, shake his hand, thank him. Cameras flash— probably from the student paper. I square my shoulders and flash the pleasant, confident smile I've honed over two decades of book tours, pretending I didn't just spend the last half-hour replaying mistakes I swore I'd buried.

Inside, the ornate foyer smells faintly of office supplies and lemon polish. The walls are lined with black-and- white portraits of past faculty, all serious eyes and high collars—people who achieved some sort of distinguished position in society or hung around long enough to become part of the scenery. A professor in a long cardigan introduces herself as Dr. Kellerman, chair of the English department. "We'll do the honorary degree presentation first," she says as she leads me up the grand staircase. "Then we'll move to the reading hall for your interview with the paper. Full house today—we have several students who are aspiring novelists. We're always so excited to have you here. Today is no exception."

I nod along, giving the right answers, smiling in the right places. But in the back of my mind, Zoe is still standing at that signing table, sliding her book toward me with that wide grin. Bridget Nelson Cooper. The name had jarred me. Bridget Nelson I knew—the girl I took to LSU football games, the girl whose hand I held on the levee. Bridget Nelson Cooper is the married version I'd seen in a handful of Facebook photos—smiling beside a tall man in sunglasses, on a beach somewhere. We are technically "friends," but Facebook is a graveyard for us, the kind of connection that exists in name only. Truth be told, I don't look that often.

Dr. Kellerman pushes open a set of double doors to a wood-paneled auditorium. Warm lighting pools over a stage with a podium and two chairs. A banner above the stage reads: ROOSEVELT COLLEGE HONORS JEFF GRIFFIN, author of the bestselling series, *Les Dossiers Blackthorn: The Casebooks of Detective Jeremy Blackthorn*. They've lined up all eight of my books on a table, the latest facing out, front and center: *No Friend but the Night*. Polite applause greets me as we step inside. I raise a hand, scan the audience, see a dozen bright young faces looking at me like I'm some combination of celebrity and prophet.

And then I see her.

Two-thirds of the way back, leaning against the wall near the exit, Zoe—hands in her pockets, half-smile on her face, arms folded protectively across her chest.

I'm seated in one of two chairs on stage, a bottle of water at my feet, the honorary degree certificate resting on my lap like a polite hostage. Beside me, the editor of the Roosevelt Herald—a junior named Owen with wire-rimmed glasses and a sharp, eager expression—leans toward the microphone.

"Mr. Griffin," he begins in a British accent, "first, congratulations on completing your series. It's been called one of the defining works of contemporary American crime fiction. Could you tell us what it feels like to let go of a character like Jeremy Blackthorn, a character you've been writing for a decade and a half?"

I give him the practiced answer—how it's bittersweet, how the characters feel like family, how endings are necessary for growth. My voice is steady, my hands loose in my lap. But from the corner of my eye, I can see Zoe still leaning against the wall, not in the polite, attentive pose of the other students, but leaning back, one foot crossed over the other, watching me like she's waiting for a different kind of performance.

Owen moves on. "Many young writers here are concerned about the future of literature, especially in an age dominated by streaming and social media. What advice do you have for those who want to keep the humanities alive?"

I launch into my philosophy—the importance of empathy in storytelling, of reading widely, of resisting the fast dopamine of a scrolling feed. It's the kind of speech that usually earns nods and applause. But mid-sentence, Zoe tilts her head, like she's hearing an entirely different conversation.

And suddenly I'm back in Carly's apartment again, ice clinking in a glass, her eyes avoiding mine. The memory of the smell of her shampoo mixing with that of the bitter coffee we drank the next morning.

"—and so my advice," I hear myself saying in the present, pulling hard on the thread of my own voice to get back on track, "is to write with the assumption that your words matter, even if the world tries to convince you otherwise."

I talk about empathy and language being the root of understanding. "Words are bridges. Learn as many as you can. Not just English — I mean other languages, other systems of thought. I studied French at LSU, and I've kept it up ever since. As a kid, I learned sign language because my best friend was deaf. Those languages shaped me as much as Faulkner or Tennessee Williams did. They taught me that there are countless ways to see the world."

The students nod, scribbling. Owen looks pleased with himself for asking the question.

And yet, while I speak about bridges and words, I can feel Zoe's gaze from the back of the room, steady and unreadable.

Owen smiles, jotting something down. "That's great. One more question—can you tell us what's next for Jeff Griffin?"

I give the obligatory shrug and hint about a stand-alone novel in the early stages, something I'm not ready to talk about in detail. But my mind's not on the book. It's on Zoe, and the fact that she hasn't moved since I walked in.

When the applause comes, I shake Owen's hand, wave to the crowd, and step offstage. Dr. Kellerman is there to thank me, students already forming a cluster for selfies.

I look past them, toward the wall.

Zoe is gone.

The students close in as soon as I step off the stage— selfies, quick questions about publishing, requests for advice. I give them my best smiles, the kind that look warm in photos. But my gaze keeps drifting toward the back of the auditorium, to the spot where Zoe had been leaning against the wall.

Gone.

I excuse myself as politely as I can, telling Dr. Kellerman I need a moment before the faculty reception. She gestures toward a side door. "The green room is just down the hall, if you'd like to sit."

I don't sit. I walk.

***

The hallway smells faintly of chalk dust and whatever they polish these old floors with. I check the stairwell. Empty. I push open a door to the foyer—just a handful of students heading toward the quad, their laughter echoing against the high ceiling.

Outside, the air is cooler now. The sun has dropped low, throwing long shadows from the elms. A few students are crossing the green, backpacks slung over one shoulder, heads bent against the wind.

No Zoe.

I head toward the front gates, scanning faces, checking the benches, the paths that wind between the buildings. Nothing.

For a moment, I stand at the top of the hill, looking down at the quiet main street beyond. I could tell myself she left, caught a train, went back to wherever she came from. But that's not what my gut says.

My gut says she's still here. Watching.

And if she's watching, then she came today for more than a signed book.

Chapter One – Eighteen Years

Back at the loft in SoHo, my phone is in my hand before I've even set my helmet down, thumb hovering over Bridget's name in my contacts. We haven't spoken in years. The last time might've been a polite "Merry Christmas" in a Facebook comment. But now, after two, no three run-ins (the bookstore, the street, and The Castle) with Zoe in less than twenty-four hours, I'm done with polite distance.

Before I even hit the call button, she's calling me. "Why, hello there," I greet her.

"Hello yourself," she says, her voice a mix of warmth and surprise.

"I was about to dial you. Are you in Bronxville?"

A short laugh. "No, Zoe goes to school up there. I'm still in Baton Rouge. She texted me when she saw you in the bookstore."

"So that's Carly's daughter, huh? Sheesh. How long has it been?"

"Eighteen years. Zoe's age. She'll be 19 in August."

I let that sit for a beat. "Right."

We talk for a long while—about nothing and everything. She sounds the same, steady and warm, with a faint southern drawl. She tells me Zoe's a freshman at Roosevelt, bright, independent, a little headstrong. She says Zoe went to my book event to surprise her, to get a signed copy because "I've been telling her about you, about us, her whole life. She was excited to finally meet you face to face."

About us. She means, me and her. Bridget. The girlfriend in college I constantly cheated on. The guilt weighs heavy in my chest. I never could understand why she kept taking me back, why I kept going back, but after graduation I think she began to have enough.

After we hang up, I stay at the kitchen table, staring at the dark windows across the room, the skyline reflecting back at me.

Eighteen years.

Bridget and I were a couple for most of our time at LSU, the breakups brief and the reunions easy. Until the last one. Thanksgiving week, eighteen and a half years ago.

That night with Carly.

The memory is jagged—whiskey, shadows, silence. Carly disappearing the next day. Me never telling Bridget.

Bridget and I tried again, one last time. She came to New York with me, lasted two weeks before packing up and flying home. I stayed. Wrote plays, washed dishes. My failed career as a playwright quickly pushed me into writing novels. The years stacked up.

And now here's Zoe. 18 years old. Bridget's goddaughter. Carly's child.

I tell myself not to get ahead of it, not to read meaning into what might be a coincidence.

But the truth is, I already have.

I wasn't the type to get drunk. Not really. Sure, I went to plenty of fraternity parties, drank my share of cheap beer, went to Tigerland like everyone else. But I never lost control. Maybe it was knowing Nancy and I came from addicts—our birth parents overdosed before we were old enough to know them. Brittany and Paul Griffin raised us better than that. They saved us. They gave us a life, one that, for all my faults, and all their faults, I had sense enough to appreciate. One drink, two drinks—that was enough. Except that night. I didn't drive, but I drank too much. Way too much.

Bridget and I had fought again. One of our endless fights about the future. I wanted New York. She wanted Baton Rouge. I wanted fame and fortune. She wanted the red ink pen of a professor grading papers. She wanted the picket fence. There was always a reason, always a trigger to explode into a fight. We'd been together most of college, but every few months it seemed like we had to test how breakable we were. That night, it felt like we were broken for good. She told me she was leaving for Lafayette, going to see her sister. I went to the bar. Whiskey, beer, more whiskey. By the time I stumbled across campus toward her apartment, the world was tilting sideways. Carly answered the door. Bridget's roommate, her best friend. She looked startled to see me, but she didn't slam the door in my face. She saw I was swaying, pale. I tried to insist I could keep walking, but then I bent over and threw up in the grass. That decided it. She pulled me inside, pointed me to the couch. I remember the scratchy blanket she laid over me.

Darkness.

When I woke, pale dawn leaked through the blinds, and my head was splitting. My mouth tasted like sand. The blanket was folded neatly beside me, as if even unconscious, I'd tried to clean up after myself.

Carly came out of her room in a silk robe, hair tousled, bare legs catching the light. For the first time in four years of knowing her, I saw her not just as Bridget's best friend, but as herself. Attractive, yes. Vulnerable, too. And I hated myself for noticing.

We sat across from each other — me on the couch, her in the armchair — drinking coffee out of oversized mugs. She told me Bridget was just as upset as I was, that maybe space would do us good. She asked about my plans. I asked about hers. She was already in grad school, pursuing a Master's in library science. Bridget was in an MFA program. I was headed up to the Big Apple to achieve glory and glamor. For the first time, we actually talked.

The day unfolded in a strange haze. Carly made breakfast. We lingered. Later we walked to the LSU lakes, stopped at

Mike the Tiger's sanctuary. By the time we ended up on the so-called "Beach" on Stanford Avenue, watching the sun sink over the lake, I wasn't thinking about Bridget anymore. Or maybe I was, and that's what made it worse.

I wrapped my coat around her. I kissed her. She kissed me back. It felt inevitable, though nothing about it was.

Back at her apartment, we kissed again. We fell on her bed.

The next morning, she panicked. Told me to leave. Made me promise never to mention it to anyone. Especially Bridget. I promised. I returned to my parents' house, had Thanksgiving dinner, the last I'd ever have with my parents, although I didn't know it at the time. I never saw Carly again. Not even on Facebook. Not so much as one of those mutual-friend "suggestions" they churn out.

Bridget came back from Lafayette, and somehow we found our way back to each other—because that's what we always did. I never told her about sleeping with Carly. I buried it, swore to myself it was a mistake that belonged to no one but Carly and me.

Eighteen years later, here I am, wondering if that "mistake" has a name.

That "mistake" may actually be the only goddamned thing in my life that ever mattered.

Chapter Two – Early Signals

I wake before my alarm, the city outside my loft on Spring Street just beginning to stir—delivery trucks rumbling down the cobblestones, the faint metallic rattle of a rolling gate from the café across the street. Morning light spills across the exposed brick wall, catching on the stack of signed hardcovers I brought home from the tour.

I lie there for a while, staring at the pressed-tin ceiling, replaying Bridget's voice from last night. *I've been telling her about you, about us, her whole life.*

That *us* clings to me like cigarette smoke.

I make coffee in the open kitchen, the French press hissing softly. I tell myself I'm heading back to Roosevelt for a perfectly normal reason—drop off pre-signed books for the student paper, maybe answer a couple more questions for their feature. Completely aboveboard.

But in truth, I want to see her again.

***

The campus is quiet when I arrive—low sun spilling over the quad, a few students crossing the grass with coffee cups and laptops. Roosevelt looks even more postcard-perfect in the morning, like it's been waiting here all night just to impress someone.

My pretext is airtight: drop off the box of signed books for the student paper and English department. Nobody can accuse me of stalking a student.

I stop by the student center, ask the kid behind the desk where I might find the Roosevelt Herald office. He recognizes me, as he attended the event yesterday. He eagerly volunteers to take me there. Owen, the editor, is excited to see me again. I hand him the box and he takes it with gratitude.

"That was very thoughtful of you, sir."

"Jeff, please."

"Right. Would you like me to show you around, take you anywhere? I could take you to Dr. Kellerman. She's the faculty advisor for the paper."

I clear my throat. "Actually, Owen, I was wondering if you might know a student here. She was at the signing in town and the interview yesterday. She had some questions for me but, I don't know, when I tried to find her to answer them she was gone."

Owen looks baffled and I don't blame him. I'm being weird. "Well, um, do you know her name?"

"Zoe MacKenzie."

"Zoe MacKenzie?" he repeats, thinking. "Yeah, the freshman. She was interested in writing for the paper but I had to explain to her that there's a requirement to be a sophomore. I have seen her working in the library. I can take you if you want."

The library is three floors of hushed air and that dry, sweet smell of paper.

I glance at Owen.

"I love libraries. Do you mind if I just walk around on my own? Browse the books?" I wink and add, with a sheepish grin, "It's a hobby of mine, my heaven."

He chuckles. "I guess not. If you need anything else, come back to the office. Anytime. I can speak for Dr. Kellerman, and I feel the same. She said it yesterday. You're welcome here anytime. You are, after all, technically an alumnus."

I chuckle at his joke about my honorary doctorate. Jesus, if people start calling me Dr. Griffin…

With Owen walking away, I climb to the second floor and spot her behind the reference desk—hair pulled back, a navy cardigan, jeans. She's scanning barcodes on a stack of returns, tapping keys without looking.

When she notices me, her eyebrows lift slightly. "Mr. Griffin. Twice in two days. Should I be flattered or concerned?"

I lean on the counter, pretending I'm just passing by. "Depends on who's asking. I came to drop something off for the student paper." The one signed book I took out of the box I gave to Owen. I slide it toward her on the counter. "Figured I'd hand-deliver this one for the library before I head back to the city."

She takes the book, glancing at the inscription. "That's very... generous of you."

"Generous is one word for it." I smile. "You work here?"

"Part-time. Helps cover books and bad coffee habits." She tilts her head. "Bronxville's not exactly a quick trip from SoHo."

Her tone is casual, but the mention of SoHo feels deliberate.

I shrug, keeping my own voice light. "Some trips are worth making."

I notice her sly look as she sets the book aside. I study her face, trying to decide if her remark was just based on a lucky guess, or if she knows more than she should.

"You've been doing your homework," I say lightly.

She shrugs. "You're not hard to find. Google is full of answers about Pulitzer finalists who write bestselling novels and do NPR interviews. You're very chatty in those interviews." A grin. "You're practically a walking syllabus."

I laugh, though it feels thin and I feel a cold ripple along my spine. "Well, writers trade privacy for readers, the way surgeons give up sleep for patients. Comes with the territory."

Zoe leans forward on her elbows. "Plus, you're not exactly invisible. Your publisher keeps you busy...and Bridget has told me a lot of stories. Is it true you studied French literature at LSU? My godmother says you carried around battered copies of Faulkner and Borges. She said you even fenced. Hard to picture a crime novelist in a mask, waving a foil."

Her tone is playful, but the fact that she knows the details—details Bridget used to tease me about—makes me feel pinned.

"True enough," I admit. "Though the fencing was mostly an excuse to look elegant while losing to better athletes. And Borges?" I smile faintly. "I thought his labyrinths would unlock the universe if I read them enough times."

She smiles. "Godmother said you were very good at pretending not to care.

The words land with a little too much weight. I change the subject fast, attempting to look neutral. "So what about you? What's your major?"

"Undecided. History maybe. Or creative writing. Depends on the semester. Depends on what feels real. Bridget thinks I've got potential as a writer."

She tucks a strand of hair behind her ear. That's when I really notice her eyes: gray like mine. Deep pools of emotion—sadness, mostly—that pierce my heart. Continuing, she says, "She teaches English now, so I can't exactly ignore her when she says it."

"Professor Nelson," I say, the title tasting strange on my tongue.

"Dr. Nelson Cooper," Zoe says, rolling the name like it's the punchline to an inside joke.

"Oh, right," I correct myself quickly. "Professor Cooper."

Zoe smirks. "Don't let her hear you call her that. She says to her students, 'There is a Dr. Cooper at LSU, but it's not me—it's my husband.' Ed is Dr. Cooper. Bridget is Dr. Nelson Cooper."

"Oh, right," I nod, as if I'd only misspoken, though the name rings like a bell I can't un-hear.

She tilts her head. "Bridget said you always had a French novel tucked under your arm too. Hugo, maybe?"

That makes me laugh. "I tried to look impressive lugging around *Les Misérables*, but truth be told, I loved it. Still do. Hunchback too."

Zoe nods. "I need to take a language for my core requirement. Was thinking French, actually."

I lean on the counter. "Take it. You'll never regret it. French taught me rhythm. And sign language taught me silence."

Her brow furrows, intrigued. "Sign language?"

"Yeah. I learned it as a kid—my best friend was deaf. It stuck."

For a moment, something flickers in her expression, quick and unreadable, before she shifts back into that half-smile.

She flips the signed book shut, tucks it under her arm. "So yeah, Bridget's the English professor, but honestly? Between her and my mom, it was like growing up in a seminar room. One had the novels, the other had the library card catalog. No escape."

She says it like a joke, but my stomach knots at the word mom.

I try to keep my voice casual. "Your mom's a librarian, isn't she?"

"Head of a special collection in the public library now," Zoe says. "Still calls herself a glorified book hoarder. Bridget used to tease her about it—'Nelson does the literature, MacKenzie does the shelves.' They make a good team."

Carly. Hearing her name spoken aloud after all these years feels like someone prying up a floorboard in a long-abandoned room. The way Zoe talks about Carly and Bridget making 'a good team.' There's a trace of bitterness in her tone that I file away, not knowing why but wanting to understand. Instinctively, it feels like a clue to the elusive puzzle called Zoe MacKenzie.

Zoe studies me again with that same half-smile from the bookstore.

For a moment, I forget where I am—the library hum, the shuffling of pages, the faint hiss of the HVAC. All I can hear is the echo of her words, and all I can see is Bridget on the LSU quad, smiling at me through sunlight, and Carly in the half-light of a Baton Rouge apartment, her silence heavier than any promise.

I clear my throat, aiming for steady. "You've got time to figure it out. Freshman year's for experimenting."

Her grin widens. "That's what I've been told." She slides the book into her bag and pushes a stray hair off her forehead. "Thanks for stopping by, Mr. Griffin. I'll tell Bridget you said hello."

And just like that, she's back behind her pile of returned books, scanning barcodes, her attention on anything but me.

I stand there a beat too long before finally turning away.

Chapter Three – Am I Yours?

I don't return to SoHo right away. Instead, I wander through the streets of Bronxville. I have no clue where I'm going, but somehow I end up at the bookstore where I did the signing yesterday. Where Zoe walked right up to me and dropped names that hit me like a punch to the gut. There's a coffee shop next to the bookstore.

It's the middle of the afternoon and the café is full of students—milk steamers hissing, laptops open, earbuds in, the smell of burnt espresso hanging in the air, muted conversations bleeding together.

And there she is. Again. Zoe. It's like there's a magnet in the cosmos, pulling us together.

She sits alone at a corner table, red earbuds in her ears, a paperback face-down beside her cup. When she spots me, she lifts her brows like she's been expecting me.

She notices me before I can decide whether to turn around. That half-smile again. "Mr. Griffin. You haunting Bronxville now?"

I pull up a chair, uninvited. "No, Miss MacKenzie. It is a nice town, though. A nice college you picked. Was it your first choice?"

Her grin widens. She sets her book aside, leans forward. And then—without a word—her hands move, quick and precise. [You said you know sign language.]

I freeze for half a second, then answer without hesitation. My fingers shape the word before I can stop myself. [Fluent.]

Her eyebrows lift. "Interesting," she says aloud, but her hands flick again, casual, quick. [Bridget never mentioned that.]

I shrug, pretending calm even as my pulse kicks. [Bridget doesn't know everything.]

She sits back, satisfied, sipping her coffee like nothing happened. To everyone else in the café, we're just another student and an author chatting about books. But between our hands, something else is alive—something private.

She signs back: [True.]

[Seems you're fluent too,] I say silently with my fingers.

She takes a sip of coffee, then lets her hands rest on the cup's cardboard sleeve. For a moment, it looks like idle fidgeting—until her fingers shape another phrase, quicker this time. [Summer camp. Mom made me go to piano camp every summer. They didn't just teach piano. Tons of electives. The other girls opted for crochet or 3D printing. I don't like crowds.]

[Piano camp, huh?] My mind instantly flashes to the piano in my loft.

[Mom's way of making sure I'm well-rounded.]

My stomach lurches. There's just something about the way she says Mom. She did it in the library too, and twice more right here. To anyone watching, she's just twirling her cup, casual as ever.

I force myself to breathe. My own hands answer slowly, carefully: [How is Carly?]

Zoe's mouth curves into that half-smile again. She leans back, taps the side of her cup with one finger. Out loud, she says, "Solid as a rock."

But with her free hand, hidden between us, she signs:

[That's what she says. Solid as a rock. She'll never show me the cracks.]

I hold her gaze, every nerve alive, my hands still on the table.

Zoe's fingers linger in that last phrase, She'll never show me the cracks.

The air between us tightens.

I open my mouth to respond, but she's already shaking her head, cheeks coloring. "This was a mistake," she mutters, snapping her book shut. The half-smile is gone. She shoves the paperback into her bag, slings it over her shoulder, and bolts.

"Zoe—" I'm up before I realize it, weaving past students and baristas, pushing through the door into the sunlight.

She's halfway down the block, moving fast. I catch up at the corner where the traffic light holds her in place. She swipes at her eyes, quick and angry, like she doesn't want me to see.

"Hey," I say softly, out of breath. "Talk to me."

"You don't get it." She keeps her back to me, shoulders stiff. "I thought—I thought maybe if I saw you, it would make sense."

Her voice cracks. She turns, eyes wet, no longer the composed girl from the signing or the smirking student behind the desk. She looks eighteen—just eighteen—and fragile in a way that cuts straight through me.

"Zoe…" My throat is tight. "What do you think you're going to find in me?"

She laughs bitterly, a shaky sound. "Answers. Or at least honesty. But maybe that's too much to ask."

She wipes her face with the heel of her hand, and it's then I see it—the exact tilt of her jaw, the way her eyes flash when she's angry. Bridget's shadow and Carly's all at once.

I want to tell her to slow down, to breathe, to sit with me until the world stops spinning. But the words that come out are simpler, truer:

"I'm here. Whatever this is, I'm not running from it."

For a second, she studies me, breath hitching, lips trembling like she's about to say something she's not ready to. She steps back, clutching her bag strap, as if the current might carry her away if she doesn't.The light changes, students surge around us, but I stay locked on her. She tries to slip away, seeming to want to fold into a group of students, but I catch her wrist—not hard, just enough.

"Zoe." My voice is low, steady. "Say it."

Her chin trembles. She shakes her head. "I can't—"

"Yes, you can." I step closer, lowering my voice so it's only for her. "Whatever you think you know, whatever you've been holding in—just say it to me. Not to Bridget. Not to your mom. To me."

Her eyes are brimming now. She yanks her wrist free but doesn't step away. "You don't understand—"

"Then make me understand."

For a long beat she just stares at me, caught between fury and grief. And then it breaks.

"My mom told me my father was some guy in Atlanta. Some old boyfriend who didn't want me. But I don't believe her." Her breath shudders out. "I think it's you."

The words hang between us, louder for us than the whole street, though she said it barely above a whisper. I feel everything go hollow—the sidewalk, the sky, the years. My heart stutters in my chest.

She swipes at her face again, looking almost defiant now. "There. I said it. That's what I've been carrying. That's what nobody will tell me."

I can't move. I can barely breathe. And for the first time I feel the secret pushing out of the dark between us — unspoken, but undeniable. The only thing I can think to do is whisper her name. "Zoe…"

She waits, eyes lock on mine, like the rest of her life depends on what I say next.

I take a step closer. She doesn't back away, but her jaw is set tight.

For a moment, silence. Then her shoulders drop and the words spill out fast and ragged:

"I've known something was wrong forever. Nobody tells me anything. Bridget treats me like I'm made of glass. Carly gets this look—like I'm a problem she has to manage. And then you show up, and suddenly everything feels like it's… about me.."

She takes a step toward me, eyes blazing through tears. We're standing mere inches apart. She whispers, "Just say it. Please. I can't stand not knowing. I can't stand being the only one who doesn't get to know the truth."

I swallowed hard, throat tight. "Yes," I said, voice rough. "Yes. You're mine."

Her face crumpled. Relief, fury, grief — all of it in one breath. She shook her head, wiping her eyes with the back of her hand. "Eighteen years," she whispers.

"Eighteen years and nobody told me. Not Carly. Not Bridget. Nobody. Do you know how humiliating that is? How much it hurts?"

"I didn't know," I say lamely. "Not until now. Not until I saw you."

She stares at me, eyes glistening, as if weighing whether to believe me. Then she whispers, "You missed everything."

For a heartbeat, something raw flickers across her face — panic, recognition, pain. Then she shakes it off, forcing a quick, brittle smile. She blinks hard to clear the tears. "Why?"

The single word burns. I have no good answer, not one that wouldn't shatter the fragile lie holding all of us together. I feel it unspooling between us: truth straining to break through.

She suddenly turns, walking away again — slower this time, as though giving me the chance to follow. And for a second I almost do. I want to. God, do I want to.

Chapter Four – Lost in the Static

Back in the city, I can't settle. The loft is all exposed brick and open rafters, loft ladder leading up to stacks of old manuscripts, and a futon I have no use for. The firehouse pole gleams in the morning light, an indulgent piece of whimsy that usually makes me smile. Tonight, it feels like a monument to the choices I made—vertical, unyielding, impossible to ignore. My apartment is so wide it echoes when I cross it. There are no walls between areas, just fat columns and some brick partitioning that wraps halfway up around the centered kitchenette. It's mainly just one huge space, three walls of brick and one side that's all windows, with sliding glass opening onto the balcony that hangs over Spring Street. My bed is in one corner, brick partitions around it and raised by two steps. There's a grand piano in another corner on the side that overlooks Sullivan Street. I bought it years ago, intending to learn to play it, but never got around to it. What have I been doing with my life? So what if I know sign language and can conjugate the verb Avoir? Everywhere around me, books, DVDs, discarded manuscripts, stacks of my own latest book, *No Friend But The Night*, #8 and final in the Detective Blackthorn series—extra copies ordered by my publisher for the book tour. My Bob Dylan vinyl collection. I've seen Bob Dylan live in Atlantic City. I don't usually go to concerts. Too loud. I thrive in the silence. At least I always told myself that. I took a model I met at a gallery opening to see Elton John at Madison Square Garden. One night at her place, never saw her again. I don't even remember her name. I've got great stories, one-offs, nothing that sticks. The piano mocks me worse than the firehouse pole. I always told myself this is my sanctuary, that I don't share it with anyone, but now it just feels like a prison, or worse...like the walls are disappearing, it's expanding, and I'm left feeling alone and hollow.

Zoe.

Eighteen years. *Les Dossiers Blackthorn.* That's what I've been doing for...almost eighteen years. Almost two decades. Not knowing about my daughter. Making up stories about a detective who lives in the night, thrives in the silence, is haunted...by women...and ghosts.

Carly. Christ.

None of this shit, none of my shit, nothing I've done means a damn thing.

I pace between the kitchen island and the windows, replaying Zoe's words. Bridget said you carried Borges. Carly handled the shelves. Bridget thinks I've got potential as a writer.

Carly's name still rattles in my head, as sharp as if she'd whispered it herself.

They make a great team, the bitterness in her tone reverberating in my head.

I pour a drink, abandon it half-finished, and check my calendar. Atlanta next: appear on CNN to talk about the book and the Pulitzer nomination. How unusual that is for noir. Afterwards, Emory, another honorary doctorate. Normally, I'd pack a bag and catch a flight, but the thought of press junkets and live shows recorded for the podcast circuit just feels unbearable now. I call my publicist and my publisher, leave messages, email the publicist, beg her to shift the CNN spot and the Emory talk to virtual. It's not about convenience—it's about what comes after. I need room to maneuver. I need to get to Baton Rouge, the place with the people who hold the answers.

My phone buzzes again and this time it's Nancy—my sister, the lawyer who manages to gossip like it's billable work. Nancy is four years older than me, but that gap has never felt like much. We were orphaned young—she was six, I was two—she remembers our bio-parents, I don't, and for a while the system could've split us apart, sent us to different homes, but we were lucky. A lawyer couple in Baton Rouge adopted us both, kept us together, raised us Catholic and comfortable. They're gone now, but we still speak of them with reverence, like saints in our own family gospel.

She's thrilled to hear I reconnected with Bridget. "I wanted you two to get married," she says, with the certainty of someone who still thinks she could've orchestrated it.

"I thought I wanted that too," I admit. "But we were always pulled in different directions."

"I see her sometimes, you know," Nancy says. "She lives in my neighborhood and they have season tickets to the LSU games like we do."

"I heard she's married now."

"Yes, a fellow professor. I can't remember what he teaches. She does English, I think."

"Kids?"

"A son, if I recall."

I stare at the rafters overhead, their dark beams cutting lines across the ceiling. "Well, I met her goddaughter."

Nancy bursts out laughing. She thinks it's hilarious. And it is—on the surface, at least. The way Zoe had introduced herself, all grin and confidence: Bridget's goddaughter.

But the word sticks in my throat now, heavier than it has any right to be. It doesn't feel like a joke anymore.

Chapter Five – The Whispering of Ghosts

The Monteleone is a shrine. Hemingway, Faulkner, Tennessee Williams—all the ghosts of Southern letters still pacing the hallways, mocking me in the gilded mirrors. I'm ordering drinks from the Carousel Bar, but I feel like an imposter. I'm no playwright, no genius. Just a crime novelist with a hole in his chest. Just an overrated noir novelist haunted not by Bourbon Street but by a girl's tears in a street in Bronxville. And here I am drinking, over drinking, just like that night. The 'mistake.' The secret. Zoe.

I'm at the rooftop pool nursing a whiskey, phone buzzing with emails from my publisher, my publicist, and CNN producers. Atlanta wants me in the studio for a book segment. Emory wants me in person for their honorary degree presentation and talk. I tell them no. I haven't got the stomach for more appearances. I'll do Atlanta virtually. I'll beam into Emory via Zoom if I must. But I need to get to Baton Rouge. I need answers.

I admit that I'm pretending to be busy while I drink more than usual. I did step out once, drifted over to a bookstore, bought a volume of Tennessee's short stories, attempting to distract my obsessive thoughts about the past, but it doesn't work. Every time I think about calling Bridget, I pour another glass instead. The booze doesn't work anymore than the short stories did. Zoe's sad eyes are swimming in my head, unshakeable. I'm haunted by my choice not to follow her. Afraid to push her away. Afraid to lose her.

Nancy calls before I can call her. She always knows. She says she heard Bridget's name in my voice before I even confirmed it. Nancy, my sister, my ballast. Sharp as glass, a lawyer who still finds any excuse and any time to gossip. It's just us now. Just us before Brittany and Paul Griffin adopted us, kept us together when the system could've easily split us apart. Just us now that they're gone, buried years ago. We still speak of them reverently and as if they might walk into the room.

She's thrilled I'm in New Orleans. Cole's thrilled too. They're driving in to see me. Dinner. They booked a room and plan to take me back to Baton Rouge in the morning. They arrive at the door to my suite looking like home. Cathartic doesn't begin to cover it. We pick a place on a narrow street where the brick sweats and the air smells like butter and old stories. The waiter pours water. Nancy studies my face the way only a sibling can.

Somewhere between the oysters and the bourbon, she says, "You're wound tight," she says. "Spill it."

I've known Nancy all my life—literally, since we were foster kids shuffled through the same broken system until Brittany and Paul Griffin had us baptized into the landed gentry of Baton Rouge. Nancy never treated me like a kid brother. We've always been a team. And right now she looks at me like she's seeing me anew.

I laugh and it sounds wrong in my throat. "Zoe."

"Bridget's goddaughter," Cole says, like he's catching up in a courtroom transcript.

"Carly's daughter," I add, because that's more to the point, and Nancy's eyes flick to mine, sharp.

"Start at the beginning," she says. "All of it."

I grip the napkin, then let go. "You know I don't get drunk," I tell her. "Never did. Birth parents OD'd, Brittany and Paul raised us better. One beer, maybe two, and never drive. I kept that like a creed."

Nancy nods. "I know."

"Except once," I say. "And now," I admit. "Been drinking like Hemingway since I saw Zoe. But I digress. Thanksgiving, eighteen and a half years ago. The last one we had with Mom and Dad. Bridget and I had that fight— the big one. She took off to Lafayette. I went to Tigerland and got wasted."

The restaurant fades a little. It's not the wine; it's Baton Rouge coming back in high relief. Last week in November, shivering because I was too drunk to think of grabbing a coat.

The sidewalk on Highland tilts under my feet. I'm twenty-two and stupid. Bridget's apartment door is a lifeboat. It opens, and it isn't Bridget. It's Carly—silk robe, bare feet, hair pulled high. She takes one look at me and says, 'You can't even stand up.' I try to be noble and throw up in the grass instead.

"Are you telling me you and Carly...." Nancy's words trail off, her eyes wide.

"One night," I say with nod. "Not that night, but the next. I showed up at their apartment. Carly let me crash on the couch. I woke at dawn. Mouth like chalk. We drank coffee, talked."

Black coffee. Her in the armchair, me on the couch. We talk like people, not orbiting satellites. About plans. Dreams. How Bridget and I keep breaking and snapping back like a bad rubber band.

Cole flags the waiter for more oysters. Nancy never looks away from me.

"Then what?" she asks.

"We walked," I say. "LSU lakes. Mike the Tiger. The Beach on Stanford. One of those strange days where time goes syrupy. By sunset I wasn't thinking with the part of me that's any good."

We're on the sand, watching the sky bruise purple. I kiss her. She kisses back. SHE KISSED BACK. We pretend the world isn't shaped like consequences. Back at the apartment we keep pretending. The next morning she panics. Tells me to go. I go.

Nancy stares at me, speechless. Cole whistles low.

Nancy's mouth twitches; she knows me.

"It was a mistake," I say as if on autopilot. "She freaked out the next morning, and I left. We made a pact never to tell anyone. I never saw her again."

Silence at the table. Only the clink of dishes and the hum of the Quarter outside.

I take a breath. "I never saw her again."

Cole exhales, low. Nancy's voice goes quiet. "You didn't tell Bridget."

"No." The word lands like a nail. "Bridget came back; we stitched ourselves together for another try. She came to New York. Hated it. Lasted two weeks, max. I stayed. The mistake went into a box with a lock."

"I've carried it around ever since," I continue after a pause. "And now Zoe shows up—Bridget's goddaughter, Carly's kid—standing right in front of me. 18 years old. What the hell am I supposed to do with that?"

Nancy leans back, arms crossed. "What you should've done a long time ago. Tell the truth. Figure out if she's yours."

Her words hit harder than the bourbon.

"She turned up at my signing in Bronxville. She was at the interview at Roosevelt. I went back to find her. I couldn't stay away. We… talked. She's sharp, Nance. Smiles like she's testing load-bearing walls. Yesterday she said it out loud on a street corner."

Nancy swallows. "Said what?"

"That she thinks I'm her father."

For a long moment all I hear is the clink of plates and the soft roar of the Quarter beyond the shutters. Cole looks away, giving us a pocket of privacy he can't actually create.

"Jeff," Nancy says, and her eyes are wet but steady, "you've been a lot of things—reckless, stubborn, romantic in the dumbest possible ways—but you've never been a coward. Don't start now."

"I don't even know how to approach it," I say. "Bridget doesn't suspect a thing. Carly told everyone the father was some guy in Atlanta who wanted no part of it. If I'm wrong, I blow up their lives for nothing. If I'm right…"

"If you're right," Nancy says, "then a girl has spent eighteen years not knowing her father because you were afraid of a story. You write difficult truths for a living. Try telling one."

The waiter sets down oysters and vanishes. My appetite doesn't show.

"I keep thinking about Brittany and Paul," I say. "How they kept us together when the system could've split us. How easy it is for a life to fork and never return."

Nancy's hand finds mine on the table. "Exactly. Don't let this fork without you looking it in the face."

I nod, once. The decision arrives like a click inside my chest.

"All right," I say. "I'll go to Baton Rouge. I'll talk to Carly. I'll tell Bridget. I'll—"

"Carefully," Nancy says. "With kindness. But yes, that's what you need to do."

Cole clears his throat. "For what it's worth, there are ways to get certainty without tossing grenades in public. Quietly. Privately. Lawyers are good for something."

"Noted," I say. "But the first thing is faces. Words. The truth in the simplest form I can say it."

Nancy squeezes my hand. "Good. Finish your oysters, Victor Hugo, and then go do the scary thing."

I try to smile. "Please. I'd rather be Tennessee."

She smirks. "Tennessee would've called those women by now, then ordered another drink."

"He's rolling in his grave either way," I say, and for the first time in days, Nancy laughs like home.

Chapter Six – Telling Hard Truths

I don't sleep much. By morning, I've already decided:
Baton Rouge.

Cole drives us back. Baton Rouge feels smaller every time,
like it's shrinking around the edges while New Orleans
sprawls outward. Somehow it's always more congested,
though. Too many cars on its horrible roads. At Nancy's
place, I lace up my old running shoes before the sun
climbs too high. Running is the only thing that quiets my
head.

The LSU lakes shimmer pale in the morning light, ducks
cutting little V-shaped waves across the surface. Sweat is
slicking down my spine as I circle the LSU lakes the way I
used to when life still felt endless. The air in Baton Rouge
is thick enough to drink and I'd been jogging since dawn.
I've got my earbuds in—Springsteen today, "Racing in the
Street"—as I let the steady thud of my feet work
something loose inside me.

I'm halfway around the bend when I see her, waiting for
me in the place we agreed to meet.

Bridget Nelson Cooper.

She's on a bench in a spot we used to claim a lot, raven-colored hair pinned back loosely, sunglasses shading her eyes. Coffee cup in hand, she's watching the ducks with that same patient concentration she used to have when she read submissions for the student editorial page.

I slow my pace to a trot, then a walk. She looks up, and for a heartbeat we are twenty again, before the fight, before the fracture.

She notices me. A flicker of recognition, then something guarded.

"Jeff."

Her voice. The same and not the same.

"Bridget," I say, closing the distance and pulling out my earbuds. I bend over, grabbing my knees in order to catch my breath. "Mind if I—?"

She gestures to the bench. I sit. We don't touch. I sit, catching my breath. The bench wood is warm from the sun.

For a moment, it's only the sound of water and birds. Ducks cut through the water in slow Vs, students drift past on bikes and rollerblades. Everything looks younger than me, except the trees.

"Still running?" she asks, not quite looking at me.

"Every morning. Keeps me sane."

She smiles faintly. "I remember. Some things don't change."

That smile stabs deeper than anything else could. "Some things do," I said.

I want to tell her about Zoe right here. About Nancy's laughter curdling into silence. About how every step I take feels like walking back through a night I can barely remember.

But I don't. Not yet.

Instead, I say, "Thanks for coming."

She studies me, finally turning her face. There's weariness there, but no cruelty.

"Of course," she says. Then: "You look tired, Jeff."

I laugh under my breath. "You have no idea."

The silence stretches. A duck quacks. Somewhere behind us, a jogger passes, feet pounding the path I'd just left.

And I know I can't carry this secret much longer.

We watch the ducks for a long minute, silence moving between us like another presence. Finally, I say it. "I have to tell you something. About Carly."

Her face turned, eyes searching mine.

"That night," I continued. "The night you went to Lafayette. I was drunk. First time in my life, really drunk. Carly let me crash at your place. And in the morning...

one thing led to another. We...." The words get stuck in my throat.

The silence is so loud it makes my ears ring. Bridget's mouth parts, then closes. She stares out at the water, gripping her coffee cup as if it might anchor her.

"You," she whispered. "With Carly."

I nod. My throat is dry, sandpaper.

Her breath catches — as if she's stricken — but she doesn't cry. She just says, flatly, "Eighteen years." Then she stands, tossing her empty cup into the bin. "19 in August," she says. I gues she's doing the math. She keeps walking down the path.

I stay on the bench, watching the ducks scatter.

***

The next morning I wake before the sun, restless. I run the streets of Baton Rouge with earbuds in, music pounding. Dylan as usual. Steeling myself to face Carly. I push harder than I should, lungs burning, sweat stinging my eyes, but it doesn't matter. I'm chasing something I can't catch. When I slow, the LSU lakes are glassy and still, the ducks drifting like scattered commas across the surface. I stop, bend double, hands on my knees. I can still see Bridget from yesterday — her face haunting my brain, that small tilt of her head when I whispered her name.

But this morning isn't hers. This morning is for Carly.

By noon I'm outside the library, changed and showered and waiting. And there she is, pushing out into the light with a stack of books pressed to her chest. She doesn't see me until I'm already moving toward her.

"Carly."

She freezes. For a moment it's as though the air thickens around her. For a second, I see her at 22 again, Bridget's roommate, silk robe, bare legs. She looks the same. Older, I guess, but barely. Something hits me in the gut when I see her—the way I used to stare at her, she'd catch me staring and look at me and laugh. God, that laugh. She's not laughing now. Her mouth hardens, rebuking me back to the present. She sets the books against her hip, jaw tightening.

"Jeff." There's no warmth in her tone.

"We need to talk."

Her grip tightens on the tote strap. Just like Zoe in that Bronxville street. "No, we don't."

She tries to move around me. I move to block her. I decide to cut to it. No rehearsed speech, no preamble. "Yes, we do. Bridget knows now. I told her. About that night. About us. And I've met Zoe."

Carly's breath hitches. Her eyes narrow. "You told Bridget?"

"Yes." My throat works. "I had to. I couldn't keep it buried anymore."

For a moment I think she might actually collapse there on the library steps. She turns away, blinking fast, then swings back with fury in her voice. "You had no right. No right to drag Bridget into this, no right to—"

But she doesn't deny it. Not once.

And that's enough.

She shakes her head, almost laughing, but it's a brittle sound. "You don't know what you've done."

"Zoe," I said. The name comes out like a plea. "She deserves the truth. So do I."

The books slip in her arms, one thudding against the steps. She doesn't bend to pick it up. "Goddamn you, Jeff."

"I had to." My voice is raw. I don't know why, but I pick up the damn book and place it on top of her stack.. "I couldn't carry it anymore. Eighteen years—"

"Don't." Her voice rises sharp, almost panicked. "Don't say it."

"Carly—"

"You don't get to walk back into town and blow up everything. You don't get to decide now, after all this time, what truths get told."

Her face is flushed, but her hands are trembling. And I know. I've known since the moment Zoe introduced herself at the signing, but hearing the anger in Carly's voice makes it real.

"She's mine," I say. Quiet. Like a confession. "Isn't she?"

The silence between us is brutal. Finally Carly exhales, a shuddering breath that sounds like surrender.

"She's yours."

***

I'm back at Nancy and Cole's mansion. They have a renovated space above the three-car garage, one of their many extravagances. Well, they need a place to put the Range Rover, the Bentley, and the Tesla. Nancy builds, Cole negotiates. They really do make a great team. Anyway, the space above the garage is a modern suite with all the creature comforts. I not only have my own kitchen up here, I've got a pool table and a patio. I'm there now, watching my nephews, Cole Jr. and Wyatt, swat at each other with plastic lightsabers in the back yard. Just now, I hear a car pull up in the driveway. It's a wraparound patio, so I move around the front of the garage, where I can see Bridget getting out of an Audi Q5. She sees me and folds her arms, looking like she's barely able to contain herself.

Nancy comes out the front door, nods at Bridget, glances up at me with raised brows, then ducks back inside.

Bridget is glaring up at me like I dragged her into a courtroom.

"You told me," she said, voice low and vibrating, "after eighteen years? After she and I raised Zoe together? After you let me believe I knew everything?"

"I thought it was better just to drop it," I say. Weak. Stupid. The truth, maybe, but flimsy as wet tissue.

She laughs once, a bitter bark. "Just to drop it? Really, Jeff? You know, it's not the fact that you jumped into bed with her less than twenty-four hours after we blew us up again. You jumped into bed with plenty of people in those days and I always forgave you. It's the fact that my best friend and my boyfriend decided to spend one night playing house, made a baby, and just acted like it was nothing."

"Bridget—"

"No." She cuts me off with a slash of her hand. "Don't 'Bridget' me. I loved you. I still —" She breaks off, shaking her head violently, as if swatting the thought away. "And you chose silence. I don't know who I'm angrier at," she said. "You, or Carly."

And then she leaves, heels striking the cement driveway like gunshots.

***

The next morning I intercept Carly again, this time outside Coffee Call. She is looking furious already, jaw tight, as if Bridget got to her first.

"You've destroyed everything," she hisses.

"I didn't destroy anything," I protest. "The truth was already there. I just—"

"You don't get it, do you? Zoe is my daughter. My responsibility. You don't just walk back into town after twenty years and decide you want answers."

I lean closer, lowering my voice. "She's my daughter too."

The words froze between us.

Carly's lips tremble, but not with hesitation — with fury. "Don't you dare say that. You gave up that right the moment you—"

"I didn't know," I say, voice breaking. "Carly, I didn't know. You never told me. If you had—"

I see the waterworks building in her eyes, but she blinks the tears away hard. "Don't you dare make this about what I did or didn't do. You left. You stayed gone. Bridget and I built a life. We raised Zoe. You don't get to show up now and unravel it because you suddenly feel nostalgic."

"I'm not nostalgic," I whisper. "I just want the truth. And, for the record, you told me to leave. You begged me."

"Well," she snaps, "congratulations. You've got the truth. And now we're all paying the price."

She storms off, tote bag swinging hard against her hip.

"Zoe wants the truth too!" I yell back.

Chapter Seven – Out of the Ruins

I couldn't stand another day in Baton Rouge. Nancy tried to talk me down, but I could feel the walls closing in — Bridget's anger, Carly's fury, Zoe's face flashing in my mind every time I shut my eyes.

I booked the first flight to New York, sat on the plane staring out the window at the clouds, wondering if I'd just detonated the only real connection I had left to Louisiana.

Back in Soho, the loft feels cavernous, all exposed brick, holding heat like a grudge, unfriendly, and mocking me with the silence that used to comfort me. The rafters creak. The emptiness closes in on me. The bricks seem to hold in more silence than I can handle. I've got the floor-to-ceiling windows open, the air thick with the early summer heat, the city hum rising up in waves. The firehouse pole gleams like an inside-joke I'm not in on anymore. I try music. It only makes the silence louder. I keep thinking if I stand in the right spot, the city will tell me what to do. It doesn't. When the bourbon does nothing, memory steps in. I'm walking the loft like a ghost, Dylan low on the stereo, thinking about how the truth is supposed to set you free. All it has done is chain me tighter.

I should be relieved to be home, but my mind keeps cycling, stuttering back over Louisiana like a broken record. Carly in the library doorway, Bridget on the bench at the LSU lakes, both of them turned to glass when I touched them with truth. Carly's face when I said it — when I admitted I'd told Bridget. Then Bridget's face later, sharper still, when she clanked up Nancy's driveway in her heels.

I see it as clearly as if I'm still there.

After Bridget drove off, I went down to the main house, found Nancy in the kitchen, wrangling with my nephews, who were sword-fighting with plastic lightsabers. I sat at the table, nursing a beer, trying to breathe. And then the doorbell sounded. I went to open the door. It was Bridget, returning to tell me off some more. She marched past me. She had that same expression from college, the one that used to subdue me: cool, steady, as if she had already weighed every word she was about to speak and found it heavier than me. My nephews came bursting out of the kitchen, their sword fight intensifying, Nancy in their wake trying to divert them.

Bridget glanced at Nancy and back at me. "You told her," she said. Not a question. Nancy retreated back to the kitchen, I know to give us privacy, which was the last thing I wanted. Wyatt's shriek, in the backyard, carried in through the open window, followed by Cole Jr. shouting, "Uncle Jeff, come play with us!" I could have kissed the kid for the interruption.

"Yes," I finally said in answer to Bridget.

She folded her arms. "After eighteen years of silence. You picked now."

"Nancy deserved to know about my daughter," I muttered. "And so did you."

Having run back in the house, one of the boys whacked my leg with his lightsaber. I grabbed it from him, twirled it once, gave him a mock-serious glare — anything to buy myself a few more seconds. Bridget just stood there. Watching. Silent. And when Nancy returned, dusting grass from her jeans, Bridget didn't even try to hide the way she was looking at me, like a man who had burned down the wrong house to keep himself warm.

I've been carrying that look with me ever since.

Now, back in SoHo, it clings to me. The loft walls don't help. Neither does the bourbon. The city feels too small for the weight of it.

So I get on the bike.

Chapter Eight – Safe Among Friends

I take the Ducati down through the tunnel and east, the Manhattan skyline shrinking in my mirrors. Queens opens up before me — low roofs, modest lawns, slices of sky I can actually see without craning my neck. I roll into Forest Hills, where the streets smell like barbecues and laundry detergent, not exhaust fumes.

Theo's place sits on a corner lot, a compact house with green grass cropped close and a baby stroller box leaning against the porch. The Ducati hum dies as I cut the engine, but the door swings open before I take my helmet off.

Theo stands there grinning, signing with exaggerated flare: [Late, Griffin. Story of your life.]

I laugh despite myself, climbing off the bike. He grabs me in a bear hug that knocks the air from my lungs.

"You smell like motor oil and marinara," I mutter, letting him read my lips. He has his own Ducati, even better than mine.

He signs back, quick and sharp: [Better than whiskey and regret.]

Theo Arceneaux and I have been best friends since the third grade. He's the friend who motivated me to learn sign language. When everyone else floated through my childhood, too fast or too busy to wait for me, Theo stayed still. His signal alone held steady. So I signed with him and we've been inseparable ever since. We even drive the same kind of motorcycle, though his is far more powerful and he takes it to a whole other level as a super moderator on an online Ducati forum. He came to New York shortly after I did, worked in publishing for a while, became a Certified Deaf Interpreter, and now he works for a disability advocacy group. He wrote a children's series about "voice", did a TED Talk, and is a fairly well-known motivational speaker. Five years ago, he married a woman from New Jersey and now they're expecting their first child.

Inside, the house feels too warm, too alive. There's spaghetti on the stove, knitted baby socks on the couch. Domesticity everywhere, radiating calm. I set my helmet down and remove my leather jacket.

Theo's wife steps out of the kitchen, wiping her hands on a towel. Julia. Julia with her dark hair tied back, her eyes calm but knowing, her hand resting unconsciously on the curve of her belly. She smiles, not the polite kind, but the kind that tells you she's already reading you before you've opened your mouth.

"Jeff," she says warmly. "Sit. Eat. Pretend we're normal for one night."

Theo signs something behind her back, smirking —
[She's the real boss here. Don't argue.]

I shake my head, but I let the smell of garlic and tomato pull me in. The clatter of plates, the light in their faces, the sound of Theo's laugh—it all makes me feel, for the first time in days, like maybe I haven't drowned yet.

For now, I let myself sit in it. The warmth. The banter. The illusion that I belong.

The plates are cleared, Julia shooing both of us out of the kitchen with a mock sternness that makes Theo grin like a kid caught stealing cookies. He guides me into the living room, flicking on a lamp that casts the whole place in a honey-colored glow.

I sink into the couch, the cushions too soft, too forgiving. Theo drops into the armchair at a right angle to where I sit, swinging one leg casually over the other, signing with deliberate slowness, the way he does when he's making sure I catch every jab.

[You ate like a man starving. What've you been doing in Louisiana—forgetting how to feed yourself?]

I smirk and sign back. [Your cooking's better.]

He snorts, signs: [Julia cooked. I supervised.]

In a mood to tease back, I give voice to the words he signed. "Jules, is it true? You cooked? He supervised?"

From the kitchen, Julia's voice floats in: "Supervised, my ass."

I sign her words to him and he winks. Then his hands move sharper, faster, the humor giving way to curiosity. [So. You've been brooding. It shows in your face. Your eyes look like unpaid bills.]

[Thanks,] I say out loud, conveying my sarcastic tone with my facial expression and touching my fingertips to my chin. I then reached for the beer bottle on the coffee table. I twist the cap but don't drink.

He leans forward. [Spill it, Griffin.]

I stare at the dark TV screen, my own reflection fractured in it. [It's complicated.]

Theo throws his head back and laughs silently, his whole body shaking. Then he signs, [You always say that. That's your catchphrase. Complicated is code for: I'm about to blow up my own life and I need you to help pick up the pieces.]

Julia steps in from the kitchen, carrying a bowl of strawberries. She sets them down and sits in the armchair opposite me so Theo is between us. Her hand is resting again on the curve of her belly. Her eyes flick from me to him, then back to me, and I realize she knows, maybe not the specifics, but, enough. She doesn't need details to sense the gist of it. I guess being a therapist gives you that ability.

Theo's hands cut the air again, softer this time. [Is it Bridget?]

I don't answer.

[Or someone else?]

The silence stretches, thick enough to choke on. Finally I let out a breath I've been holding since Baton Rouge. [It's… someone else. And also Bridget. And everything in between.]

Theo whistles low, the sound oddly sharp coming from him. Then he grins, wide and merciless, his eyes gleaming. He signs with both hands at once, exaggerated, like he's on stage: [Of course it is. Because you, my friend, do not know how to do simple.]

Julia laughs, shaking her head, though her gaze on me softens. "Whatever it is, Jeff—you're among friends. So sit there and stew, or talk. Either way, we're not letting you leave until you unclench a little."

I lean back into the couch, beer still untouched, and close my eyes. Their voices, their presence, the warmth of this small house—it presses against me like a balm.

I take a long breath. The bottle in my hand sweats against my palm. "All right," I say. "You asked for it."

Theo grins, leaning back like a man settling in for a movie. Julia tucks her legs under her on the sofa, the therapist in her already reading my face like a patient file.

"It started with Zoe," I say, signing and talking at the same time. The name feels heavy, dangerous in the air. "A girl I met at a book signing. She came up to the table, rattled off her godmother's name, like she knew exactly how to punch me in the gut. And when she looked at me…" I pause. The living room fades, replaced by the bookstore in Bronxville—the line of eager readers, the overhead lights glaring, her dark eyes locking on mine. "Something cracked open. I knew. Didn't want to, but I did."

Theo tilts his head. [Knew what?]

I swallow. [That she was mine.]

Julia's hand stills on her belly. The room goes quiet except for the faint hum of the refrigerator.

I keep going before I can stop. "After that, I couldn't stay still. I flew down to New Orleans, I went to Nancy, to clear my head. But the past kept chasing me. Carly—Bridget's old roommate. One night, years ago, after Bridget and I had split—briefly—I got drunk, for the first time in my life. Carly let me crash on her couch. By morning, I started to cross a line I couldn't uncross."

The memory blooms, unbidden: a shabby college apartment, the smell of stale beer, Carly in a silk robe, pouring coffee while my head pounded. That long day at the LSU lakes, sunlight bouncing off the water, walking the trail, talking about futures we never committed to. Her bare feet in the sand, the heat of her mouth against mine at sunset. I squeeze my eyes shut, willing it away.

Theo's signing slows. [You're telling me...this Zoe—] he gestures, shaping the name in the air—[she's from that night?]

"Yeah," I whisper. "She's Carly's. She's mine."

Julia lets out a sharp breath, but says nothing. Theo just studies me, eyes dark but not unkind.

I push forward. "I told Nancy first. Over dinner with her and Cole. Then I called Bridget, met her at the lakes. Then Bridget cornered me at Nancy's house, with my nephews running around the yard. She wanted answers I couldn't give cleanly. I told her about Carly, about Zoe. And she… she turned on Carly more than me. Like betrayal stung worse coming from her best friend."

I see it again: Nancy's boys darting across the grass, shouting and swinging lightsabers, while Bridget's voice hissed in my ear—accusing, disbelieving, her face pale with fury. Carly's face when I confronted her, the way she finally admitted what I already knew, her eyes blazing as she said Zoe was mine.

I rub a hand across my face. "They were both furious. Carly, because I broke the silence. Bridget, because Carly never told her. And me? I just… I ran. Caught a flight north before I torched everything worse than I already had."

The room settles into silence again. Julia watches me like she's piecing together a puzzle with too many jagged edges. Theo, though—Theo smiles faintly. Signs: [So. You found your limit. At last.]

I laugh, a bitter little sound. "Feels more like I lost it."

Theo shakes his head. [No. You're still here. Means you didn't lose it yet.]

Julia squeezes his hand, then looks back at me. "So what now?" she asks softly.

I don't have an answer.

Chapter Nine - Learning to Stay

The next morning sunlight slants across Julia's kitchen table. She's humming while she butters toast, moving carefully, the kind of grace you only notice in someone carrying new life. For a minute I let myself sink into it— the smell of coffee, the soft clink of dishes, Theo's Ducati coughing to life in the driveway like it's clearing its throat before roaring. For a minute I pretend I could stay here forever, a ghost among the living, and no one would come looking.

Then my phone buzzes. Unknown number. I let it die in my pocket. Thirty seconds later it rings again.

I answer. My voice is rough. "Yeah?"

"Mr. Griffin?"

Her voice. Young, taut with nerves but steadier than I expect. I don't expect the sharp inhale, the pause, the voice steady but vibrating with nerves. "This is Zoe MacKenzie. Bridget gave me your number. I didn't give her much of a choice."

I can't speak. My throat locks up.

"I'm tired of being lied to," she says. "You knew. From the start. That's why you followed me in Bronxville. That's why you looked at me the way you did."

Sharp intake of breath. Julia hears me and stops moving, a mug half-raised, eyes on me. Then, mercifully, she turns away and runs water in the sink, giving me privacy without leaving the room.

Zoe's voice sharpens. "I think we should meet. Not Bridget. Not Carly. Just us. I want the truth. From you."

My hand is slick on the phone. My pulse is hammering so hard it almost drowns her out.

"Zoe..." I whisper. I almost drop the damn phone. "You— how did you—?" I run a hand through my hair, press my palm to my eyes. "Bridget gave you my number."

"She didn't want to," she snaps. "But I made her. I'm tired of being treated like a child. I'm tired of everyone keeping things from me."

Her anger is brittle, but beneath it, I hear what's really there: hurt. Confusion. A need that mirrors my own.

"Where are you?" I ask, my voice low, steady.

"Washington Square. At the fountain."

"Stay there," I tell her, sounding rougher than I intend.

I grab my jacket, my keys. The door slams behind me. I barely acknowledge Theo in the driveway, working on his Ducati as I mount my own. I can feel him gaping at me.

By the time I get there, the park is buzzing with students and tourists. The fountain sprays fine mist onto the pavement. And there she is—perched on the edge of the basin, hunched forward, arms crossed against the wind.

For a moment, I just stand there. I see the child she must've been, the young woman she's becoming, and the impossible truth between us. My throat is dry, my chest too tight.

She looks up. Our eyes lock. There's no escape now. I don't want to escape. I want to plunge in.

I walk to her, each step heavier than the last. She doesn't move. Doesn't flinch. Just watches me, like she's measuring the man she's been told about against the one standing in front of her.

I sit down beside her, not too close. The spray of the fountain dapples my sleeve. My hands feel useless.

"Why didn't anyone tell me?" she asks, voice breaking.

I close my eyes. The words taste like rust in my mouth. "Because we were cowards. Because I was an idiot."

Her head jerks toward me, sharp. Her eyes glisten in the lamplight. "So it's true?"

And I know there's no hiding anymore.

"Yes," I whisper. "It's true."

She's staring at me, fists clenched, the fountain spray catching her braided hair and sparkling in the sunlight.

My confession hangs between us, raw and jagged. I feel the park pressing in—the strangers, the chess players.

"Walk with me," I say.

Her brows knit. She doesn't move.

"Please," I add. Not a command. A plea.

I stand, step just far enough that she'll have to choose to follow. After a beat, curiosity wins. She pushes off the fountain ledge and comes with me, her sneakers scraping against the pavement.

I stay close, hovering at her side. My hand hangs between us like it has its own gravity. Finally, I offer it. She recoils, sharp, shaking her head.

But I don't let go; I hold her with my eyes. I lock on hers, silently imploring her to trust me.

She exhales, sharp and annoyed, but her fingers slip into mine. Small, tense, trembling. I close around them, steady. Not forcing—just guiding.

At the curb, my Ducati waits like a coiled animal. Her eyes widen when she sees it.

"You ride?" she asks, disbelief thick in her voice.

"Yeah." I hold up my helmet. "Here. Put this on."

She shakes her head. "No, I don't—"

"Zoe. Please. I need you safe."

Something in my tone silences her protest. She slips the helmet on. It's too big for her, and for a moment she looks impossibly young. My chest aches.

I swing my leg over the bike, steady it as she climbs on behind me, stiff as a board. When I feel her hesitate, I reach back, press her arms around my waist. "Hold tight."

The Ducati growls to life, and we cut through the city, weaving around the traffic. Her grip is rigid, like she's trying to resist me even as she clings.

I don't take her to the loft. Not yet. Instead, I pull up outside a corner diner, warm light spilling onto the sidewalk. I kill the engine, pull off my gloves, and help her off with the helmet.

She looks around, confused. "What are we doing here?"

"Feeding you." I nod toward the door. "You look like you haven't been taking care of yourself."

Her eyes flash. "Don't start being all fatherly now. You don't get to do that."

I take the hit, swallow it down. "Maybe not. But you're still eating."

She rolls her eyes, mutters something under her breath, but her stomach betrays her with a low growl. She tries to cover it, cheeks coloring. I open the door, stand back.

"After you."

She huffs, annoyed, but steps inside. Hunger wins.

The place is small, crowded, and smells of sizzling bacon and burnt coffee. Couples lean close across their tables, voices hushed and intimate. The regular customers are gathered at the counter, a few hiding behind newspapers. A low hum of jazz leaks from hidden speakers. I guide Zoe to a two-top against the wall, where I can keep my back to the room and her in clear view.

She drops into the chair, arms folded, chin tilted, looking every inch her mother at 18. Carly with my eyes. A blade of memory cuts me so deep I have to clear my throat before I can speak.

The waiter comes. I order two plates without asking her. Scrambled eggs, hash browns, and sausage. She glares.

"I can order for myself," she says.

"I know," I reply evenly. "But you wouldn't. You'd ask for a coffee and pretend you weren't hungry."

Her jaw tightens, but she doesn't correct me.

When the waiter leaves, she drums her fingers on the table, eyes darting everywhere but me. Finally, she pins me down. "So. You're my father. Just like that. Congratulations."

The sarcasm is acidic and it burns. I force myself not to flinch.

"I didn't know," I tell her quietly. "Not for certain. Not until I saw you."

Her lips twitch—like she almost believes me—but then she shakes her head. "Eighteen years. You never thought to check? To ask? To—"

"I should have." The words grind out of me. "I should have done a lot of things differently."

Her eyes search me, furious but—underneath—starved for something I can't quite name.

The food comes. The smell fills the space between us. She stares down at her plate like it's a trap. Then she picks up her fork and takes a bite of sausage.

I let myself breathe.

Halfway through the meal, her guard slips. She eats faster, almost ravenous, like she hasn't sat down to a proper dinner in weeks. When she notices me watching, she stiffens again.

"Don't look at me like that."

"Like what?"

"Like you care."

I put my fork down. "Zoe, I do care. More than you know."

Her eyes blaze. "Then where the hell were you?"

The room around us fades. Just me and her, knives in every word, but something binding us too—blood, recognition, the simple inevitability of it.

She eats. Not fast this time, but steady, deliberate, eyes fixed on the plate as if the food itself offends her. I don't push conversation. I don't even pretend. I sip at my water, let the ice melt slow against my tongue, and watch her in stolen glances.

When she finally lays her fork down, she won't meet my eyes. I ask for the check, slide the card across the table, and stand. She follows, wordless, tension radiating off her like heat.

The city outside is all noise and blur. She keeps a few steps behind me, arms crossed tight, as if to remind herself this isn't trust, it's curiosity. That's all.

From the underground garage of the Shelley where I've parked the bike in my spot, I hold the elevator door for her. She steps inside, wary, like she's boarding a ship that might sink any second. The ride up is short but claustrophobic—the old cables groaning, the light flickering once, her reflection in the warped metal walls staring back at me like an accusation. Neither of us speaks.

Then the gate rattles open on the fifth floor and I lead her down the narrow hall. I push open the door to the loft and she pauses in the threshold.

It always feels bigger with someone else seeing it for the first time. The tall windows, the wide expanse of books and records, the brick walls lined with shelves and notes and half-finished manuscripts. A whole life lived in stacks and scraps.

Her eyes grow wide for half a heartbeat, just enough to betray her. Then she smothers it under a smirk.

"So this is your bachelor pad?" she says, eyes flicking over the books stacked in tottering piles, the desk littered with notes, the unmade bed tucked in the corner as though I never expected company.

Her tone is dry, a little too sharp, like she wants to prove she's unimpressed.

I let the corner of my mouth twitch, just barely. "If that's what you want to call it."

Inside, I'm rattling. Because the truth is, I don't bring people in here, not even Theo or Julia. I go to their house, but my apartment is...well, it's just my bachelor pad, with creaky rafters and a firehouse pole that stands in judgement of my reclusive, cowardly self for the last eighteen years.

What I don't tell her—what I've never told anyone—is that no woman (except Julia and Nancy) has ever been here. I've had dates, sure. A string of them, if I'm honest. But always using their place, their kitchen, their bed. I never invited them into mine. Not once. Eighteen years of writing, drafting, editing, scratching at the page until my fingers cramped. Eighteen years of late nights and early mornings, pretending that the work was enough. Pretending I was whole.

And now here she is, standing in the middle of it, close enough to touch the spine of the life I've been guarding like a secret.

She crosses her arms, lets her gaze drift up the brick walls and the high windows. "So this is your bachelor pad?" she says again, this time with a little smirk, like she's already filed me under cliché.

I shrug, leaning against the desk. "It's just a place to sleep. And write."

Her eyes linger on the towers of books, the scuffed leather chair by the window, the stacks of yellow legal pads with my handwriting filling every line. I catch it— her awe, quick as lightning—but she buries it under a scoff. "Looks like you've been auditioning for the role of tortured artist."

"I got the part," I say. My voice is even, but I don't look away from her.

She turns, pacing the floorboards, running her hand along the back of the chair, but never letting it settle. "Well, congrats. Eighteen years of...what? Being untouchable?"

"Untouched," I correct her softly.

She shoots me a glance, sharp enough to cut, but I hold it. I don't flinch. I just stand there, letting her see that I'm not going to fold or retreat into silence.

The tension builds like a storm cloud, and I can feel the crack coming. She wants to keep me at arm's length, but she's running out of room.

She lingers at the shelves, pretending to read spines, but I see her shoulders tightening with every step. She's not browsing, she's buying time.

"You know," she says finally, "this is exactly what I pictured. Some Manhattan loft where you sit alone, drinking whiskey and brooding over your genius. You probably even play jazz records at night."

"I don't drink much," I answer. Liar. I used to not drink much. Nowadays, since my signals started going haywire and all I could think about was Zoe and her sad eyes, I've been drinking nonstop. "And the music depends on the day."

"Of course it does." She says it like an accusation, but her voice is too thin to carry the weight.

I step toward her. Not much—just enough so the air between us changes, turns charged. She notices. She presses her hand flat against the bookshelf, as if she could steady herself on it.

"You think you've got me figured out," I say quietly. "But you don't know the half of it."

Her chin lifts, defensive. "Why would I want to?"

I let the silence stretch until it aches. "Because you came here."

That stops her. Her lips part, then close. She's cornered herself, and she knows it.

"You could've walked away in the park," I remind her, softer now. "You didn't. You could've eaten and gone home. But you followed me here. You want something. Even if you hate that you do."

Her jaw tightens. She turns away, pacing the length of the room, as if the wide loft has suddenly shrunk. "Don't start acting like you know what I want. You don't get to play father now, after—after all this."

The words splinter at the end, and that's the first real crack. A tremor in the wall she's been holding up.

I don't move closer. I stay where I am, anchored, letting her see that I'm not going anywhere.

"Then tell me what you want," I say. My voice is steady, but low, almost a whisper. "I'll listen. I'll stay right here and listen."

Her hands clench into fists at her sides. She looks at me, furious, frightened, and something else. And I know—it's only a matter of time before the tide comes all the way in.

She won't look at me now. She keeps circling, tracing invisible borders along the walls, like a trapped animal testing for a way out.

"You think silence is noble, don't you?" she says suddenly, not facing me. "You just sit there with your wise eyes, waiting for me to fall apart. That's your trick. Just... outlast everyone else."

I don't answer. Because she's right. Because she's seeing me clearly.

She laughs, sharp and bitter. "God, it must be so easy for you. All those books, all those awards, hiding up here while the rest of us—" She cuts herself off, teeth sinking into her lip.

I let the words hang. I want to reach for her, but I don't. Not yet.

"You don't get to stand there like you're some kind of savior," she snaps, turning on me now, her eyes bright and wet. "You don't get to act like—like any of this is about me."

Her voice cracks on that last word. That's when I know the tide's at her chin. One more swell and she's under.

I draw in a breath, slow, steady. "It is about you."

That undoes her. She flinches, as if I've struck her. Then she spins away again, pacing faster, her fists hitting her thighs with every step.

"Stop it," she says. "Stop talking like that. You don't get to —" Her voice dies. She grips the back of a chair, shoulders trembling.

I stay rooted. The air is heavy, electric. Any sudden move will scatter the ions.

But I can feel it—she's right at the edge of the break.

Her knuckles whiten on the chair, and for a second I think she'll fling it across the room. But then something shifts —her grip falters, her shoulders curl in, and she folds down on herself, sliding to the floor as if gravity finally remembered her.

Her arms come up around her knees, and she hides her face, rocking once, twice, a ragged sound tearing out of her chest. Not words—just a keening, raw and small.

I want to go to her. Every muscle in me screams for me to go to her. But I know this much: if I lunge, she'll run. So I stay where I am, my back pressed to the brick wall that divides the den from the centered kitchen, my breath shallow.

"Zoe…" Her name slips out, hushed, before I can catch it.

She flinches like her name on my lips burns her, but she doesn't move away. Doesn't run.

Her voice, muffled against her knees: "I don't know what you want from me."

My throat tightens. "Nothing."

She lifts her head, eyes rimmed in red, shining wet. "Then why—why are you doing this to me?"

I kneel, slow, careful, keeping space between us. "Because you deserve the truth. Even if it hurts. Even if it breaks both of us."

She shakes her head hard, burying it again. "I can't—I can't do this."

Her body curls tighter, like she's trying to disappear into herself. And in that collapse—wanting out, wanting in, no direction safe—I see it: the child still inside her, cornered and furious, but so desperately in need of someone who will not leave.

I shift closer, one knee touching the hardwood, but I don't close the gap. Not yet.

"Zoe," I murmur, softer this time. "Can I sit here?"

She doesn't answer, just shrugs against her knees. I take it as a fragile yes and lower myself until I'm on the floor a few feet from her, the boards cold beneath me.

Her breathing is ragged, uneven. I wait. Seconds stretch. Then, quietly:

"Can I... put my hand down? Not on you. Just here." I show her, palm open, flat against the floor between us. Neutral. A marker of presence.

Her eyes dart to it, wary. Then back to her knees. But she doesn't tell me no.

"Can I stay?" My voice breaks a little.

A shiver runs through her shoulders, and she nods, almost imperceptible.

I inch closer—an inch, no more. Her whole body recoils at the movement, but I stop immediately, hands up in surrender. "Only if it's okay," I say.

Her throat works. "Why are you asking?"

"Because I don't want to take anything from you," I tell her. "Not space, not safety. Not ever."

She stares at me then, tears making her look younger and sharper all at once. "Nobody ever asks."

The words slice me open.

I swallow hard. "Then let me be the first."

For the first time, she doesn't shrink from my gaze. She just looks—wounded, unsure, but looking. And that, in itself, feels like a permission I can barely breathe through.

I ease my palm a little closer across the floor, slow enough she could stop me with a single word. I don't reach for her. I just leave it there, open, the space between our hands no more than a breath.

Her eyes flick down, sharp, then away. Her jaw tightens. I don't move. I don't even exhale too loud.

"I'm not—" Her voice cracks. She shakes her head. "I'm not ready for this."

"I know," I whisper. "That's why I'm not asking for more. Just... let it be here."

My hand, her choice.

Her shoulders quiver. She draws in a ragged breath and lets it out like it hurts to let go of the air. For a long moment she sits, frozen, locked inside herself. Then, almost like she doesn't realize she's doing it, her fingers slide across the boards—hesitant, trembling—until they brush mine.

Not a grasp. Not even a full touch. Just a graze, feather-light.

I don't close over it. I don't dare. I let it rest there, skin to skin, fragile as glass.

Her lips part as though she's about to pull back, but instead she squeezes once—so faint I almost imagine it. A test, maybe. Or a plea.

I hold still, steady, letting her feel the weight of my silence, my patience. Staying.

"See?" I say at last, low. "You're the one who decides."

She shakes her head again, but this time it's different. Less denial, more disbelief. A tear slips down, catching in the corner of her mouth. She wipes it away roughly, but she doesn't move her hand.

And so we stay there—two people on the floor, the air thick with things neither of us can say yet—our hands not entwined but touching, barely, like an unspoken promise.

Her head dips, her lashes fluttering. She's fighting it, the way the body fights sleep when the heart is still thrashing, but her limbs betray her.

"Come on," I murmur, rising slowly, offering my hand as I did in the park.

This time she doesn't argue. She leans, heavy with the weight of too many sleepless nights, too many truths pressing in at once. Her shoulder lands against me. I steady her, just holding her upright.

Then she sags all the way in, her strength gone. I don't think about it—I just slide an arm under her knees, another around her back, and lift.

She's lighter than I expected, or maybe I've just carried her in my mind so long that the reality feels insubstantial. Her hair brushes my chin as I carry her across the open space, past the tall windows and the shadows cast by the rafters.

The bed is unmade—sheets twisted from mornings I woke alone, always alone. I set her down gently, careful as if she might shatter. Her eyes open for the barest flicker, cloudy, then close again.

I kneel, unlace her shoes, slide them off one at a time. She makes the smallest sound—half sigh, half protest—but doesn't rouse. I tug the blanket loose, cover her, tuck it around her shoulders.

There she is. Breathing steady, mouth parted, a faint crease between her brows even in sleep, as though she's bracing for some blow.

I sit on the edge of the mattress, watching, my hand hovering but not daring to touch. Just watching, and listening.

Eventually the storm in my chest forces me up. I pad across the loft in bare feet, the boards creaking under me.

In the kitchen I reach for the bourbon, pour two fingers neat. The glass clinks soft against the counter. Christ, it's not even noon.

I take a slow sip, eyes closed. The burn steadies me, a reminder that I'm still here, still tethered, though the ground beneath me feels like it's shifting with every breath she takes.

Afternoon sunlight cuts across the loft in wide bands, warming the brick. My neck aches. I must have dozed off in the chair, bourbon glass still on the table beside me, the bottle half-drained. I really need to nip these new drinking habits of mine in the bud. I'm losing control.

The first thing I notice is the bed. Empty.

My chest seizes. I'm on my feet before I'm awake, the panic flaring raw and fast. Did she slip out? Did I let her—

Then I catch it: the faint gurgle of the coffeemaker. The smell of it rising, bitter and grounding. I turn, and through the open doors I see her—barefoot on the patio, cradling a mug in both hands, hair loose, face lifted toward the skyline.

She hasn't run.

I breathe again.

For a moment I just stand there in the doorway, taking in the sight of her against the sprawl of the city, so impossibly at ease, as if she's always belonged here.

She doesn't see me until I step out. Then she half-turns, shielding her eyes from the light with the rim of the mug. "Your coffeemaker's stubborn," she says. "But I won."

Her tone is wry, guarded. Still, she's here.

I lean against the rail beside her, keeping space between us, letting the quiet settle. "You gave me a scare," I admit. My voice comes rough. "Woke up and the bed was empty."

Her smirk softens, just barely. She takes another sip, eyes drifting back over the skyline.

I don't press. I just stand there with her, the city humming below, the space between us alive with everything unsaid.

"Coffee's not enough," I tell her. "You need food."

She gives me a look, half amusement, half suspicion. "What are you, suddenly my nutritionist?"

"Waffles," I say simply. "It's one of the few things I can do right. In fact, some say my waffles are the best thing I do."

That earns me the ghost of a smile. She shrugs. "Waffles better than the Blackthorn novels?" A joke about my noir books: *Les Dossiers Blackthorn*. God, I hope she hasn't read them.

I shrug. "My friend Theo has one word for my waffles: legendary."

Back in the kitchen, I pull out the waffle maker. I'm not a cook. I only know a few things: waffles or toast, pasta, chili, mac and cheese. I can make a decent vegetable stew, cook lentils, roast vegetables. That's about it. If I'm in the mood for anything else, I get takeout. Bachelor pad life. That's me. Cliche.

She hovers near the counter, pretending indifference, but I can feel her eyes on me.

When I set the plate in front of her, waffles drizzled in maple syrup, she stares at it like she doesn't quite trust it. Then she picks up her fork, takes a bite....

Her eyes flicker wide, then narrow again fast, as if she doesn't want to give me the satisfaction. "Okay," she admits. "This isn't... it's not terrible."

I laugh quietly. I made some for myself too, but I enjoy watching her eat. It's amusing to see her denying how hungry she is until, halfway through, she can't deny it anymore and her pace quickens. I slow myself deliberately, just taking occasional bites as I observe her losing the battle against her own appetite.

For a few minutes the tension eases, not gone, but softened by full stomachs. Two people at a kitchen table, pretending to be normal.

She eats until her plate is nearly clean, then pushes it away like she's caught herself giving too much. "Don't get used to this," she says.

"I wouldn't dare."

The air tightens again. I take a bite of waffles and give her space. Outside the patio doors the city is in full swing, all horns and engines and the faint whistle of a street vendor. For a heartbeat it feels like a life I might've had: waffles on a Sunday afternoon, and someone at the table. My daughter.

She cuts through it like glass. "Don't think waffles erase eighteen years."

I nod and take the hit, sighing. "I don't."

Her fork clinks against the plate as she sits back. "Good. Because I'm not your daughter just because you can cook...really good waffles."

I open my mouth, then stop, a smile tugging at the corner of my mouth. She's right — this isn't lunch, this isn't forgiveness. It's just fuel. I sit there, holding onto the last wisps of warmth as she turns away, the city light catching in her hair.

I don't answer her. Words feel like traps right now. Julia's voice floats back to me: stand still, learn to stay in place.

I push back from the table, walk to the kitchen, open the drawer where I keep odds and ends. My hand closes on the cool metal. A single key.

When I return, she's watching me with that same wary defiance, arms crossed, ready to flee or fight. I set the key on the table between us.

"You don't have to use it," I say. My voice is even, low. "But it's yours. This place is open to you, always. I'm here when you need me."

She looks at the key as if it might burn her fingers. Then back at me. A hundred emotions flicker across her face, none of them landing. She doesn't touch it.

I don't press. I just leave it there, a small gleam of trust on the wood between us.

She doesn't move at first. The key just sits there between us, sharp-edged in the morning light. I sip my water and wait.

Finally she pushes back her chair, stands, restless. She paces the length of the loft, arms folded tight across her chest.

"You don't know what it's like," she blurts. Her voice wavers but hardens again. "To be Carly's angel. To be the perfect little girl she could hold up to everybody and say, 'look how good I did, look how good she turned out.'" Her laugh is sharp, bitter. "Except I wasn't perfect. I wanted —" She cuts herself off, rubs her face, turns away.

"What did you want?" My voice is steady, careful.

She spins back, eyes blazing. "I wanted my father. I wanted the truth. I wanted someone who wasn't looking at me like I was proof of anything."

The words hang in the air. She looks stunned that she actually said them aloud.

Her gaze drops back to the table, to the key glinting there. For a long moment she doesn't move. Then, almost angrily, she snatches it up and closes her fist around it, as though taking it is both surrender and rebellion at once.

"I'm leaving now," she says. Her chin is high but her voice cracks just slightly.

I nod. I don't try to stop her. I just let the silence carry her out the door.

She moves toward the bed where her shoes (converse) are lined neatly beneath the frame, the crossbody bag slung over the desk chair where I set it last night. She bends to put on the shoes, fingers fumbling with the laces as though every small motion carries too much weight.

I don't move. I just watch.

She slips the bag over her shoulder, squares herself, and walks to the door. She doesn't look back, not once. The door closes softly behind her.

I wait until I hear the elevator rumble and fade. Then I cross the loft, slide open the balcony doors.

From the railing, I spot her emerging on the street below, shoulders hunched, moving fast toward the subway entrance on the corner. The crowd swallows her quickly. For a moment, her hair catches the light. Then she's gone.

The city noise rises to fill the space she leaves behind.

Chapter Ten – Stories and Wounds (Zoe POV)

The subway rumbles beneath my feet as I walk, but I don't hear it as much as I feel it, a dull pulse in the concrete. What I feel more is the stupid key burning a hole in my pocket. I shouldn't have taken it. I should've left it on his counter, next to the empty bourbon glass and half-empty bottle he thinks I didn't notice.

But when he held it out, I couldn't say no. Not to him, not with those eyes that looked like they'd already lost me.

I told myself it didn't mean anything. Just metal, just a door. But my hand closed around it anyway.

I walk faster, crossbody bag slapping against my hip, like if I keep moving I can outpace the mess of this morning — the silence over waffles, the way he tucked me in like I was a kid, the way his apartment was too big and too lonely for someone who supposedly has everything.

And then there's him watching me. I feel it — even with my back turned, even with my sneakers on the sidewalk, I felt his eyes from that balcony above.

I don't know what I want. That's the problem.

I want to hate him. That would be easy. Carly deserves my hatred, Bridget too. But when I opened my mouth last night, nothing came out the way I rehearsed it in my head. Instead I just… cracked.

And he didn't flinch.

Nobody in my life lets me crack. I'm supposed to be Carly's angel, the smart girl, the funny one at Thanksgiving, the "goddaughter" with manners. Every word I say is supposed to be polite, palatable, tucked in like the corners of a bed.

But last night he let me be messy. And it scared me more than anything.

I duck into the subway entrance, swipe my metro card, and push through the turnstile. The roar of the train is a relief. It covers the sound of my thoughts, even though they're still there, pounding, overlapping.

Why did I go with him?

Why did he give me a key?

Why do I feel safer around him than I should?

And underneath all that, quieter, sharper, more dangerous:

What if I want to go back?

***

The train rocks me all the way back to campus. By the time I climb the hill to the dorm, my shoes are damp from last night's rain, my hair frizzed, my brain running on fumes. It's Sunday, thank God, no classes, no Carly hovering with that tight smile she saves for me, no Bridget trying too hard. Just the suite, the girls, and the hum of campus easing into spring.

Our suite door is cracked. Jess and Casey, no doubt, have the music on full blast, painting their nails or whatever they do on Sunday evenings. My room is mercifully untouched, bed still made, desk neat. I drop my bag, peel off my shoes, and stand there, not sure if I want to collapse or scream.

The key is still in my pocket. I slide it out, stare at it, shove it deep into my desk drawer, slam it shut.

There. Out of sight, out of mind.

Except it isn't.

I'm pacing the common room while the others chatter about some party off-campus they went to last night. I can't take the noise, the easy laughter, like everyone else got the handbook for being young and unbroken and I missed the distribution.

So I drift downstairs. Past the vending machines, the peeling flyers for poetry slams and volunteer drives, until I reach the ground floor apartment tucked in the corner.

Dr. Lawson's door is open, as it usually is on weekends. Her ground-floor apartment always smells like books and lemon pledge, as if history itself had a housekeeping schedule. Dr. Allison Lawson sits surrounded by teetering stacks—hardcovers piled on the floor, papers spread across the coffee table, a sprawl of history journals spilling from the couch cushions. She's in socks and wearing a long cardigan, hair swept into its usual messy knot. Twice divorced, no kids, and openly amused by both facts, she long ago traded personal entanglements for her students and her stories.

She gestures with her tea mug the moment I hover in the doorway. "Don't loiter, MacKenzie. You'll spook the dust motes. Come in. Sit," she says, with the easy authority of someone who's taught hundreds of half-formed adults to think in straight lines.

I step over a precarious pile of biographies and drop onto the couch, careful not to send papers sliding. The cushions smell faintly of old books, which makes sense because she practically lives in the archives.

She watches me with that look she has—not pity, never that, but appraisal, like she's tracing a through-line in a primary source.

"You've been circling history courses," she says. "Any closer to deciding on a major?"

I shrug, picking at a loose thread on my sleeve. "I like stories, I guess."

"Not stories," she corrects gently. "Histories. Which is another way of saying you like truth. Even when it's messy."

That stings harder than I expect. My throat tightens. I think of last night, of Jeff's face when I cracked open, of how much mess I've kept hidden.

Dr. Lawson tilts her head, studying me. "You want to tell me what's really bugging you?"

I almost laugh. If she knew. If she had any idea what truth I've been chasing, what truth might already be standing too close, breathing the same air.

Instead I shake my head. "Not today."

She doesn't push. She never does. Just nods, like she knows more than she lets on, and sips her tea.

For a second I wish I could spill it all right here, in this safe little apartment with the lemon cleaner smell and the old books. But then the image of his eyes holding mine comes back, and the key in the drawer upstairs, and I swallow it down.

"Not today," I repeat, softer this time.

"You look restless," she says. "Restless is usually good for essay writing. Terrible for sleep."

Her tone is dry, amused, not maternal. That's why everyone comes to her—she doesn't coddle, she cuts through.

She rises and pads into the kitchenette, sets water boiling in an old enamel kettle. "Tea? You look like you could use something steady."

"Sure."

While she moves about, I reach toward the nearest stack, fingers brushing the cracked spine of a biography of

Eleanor Roosevelt. I flip it open. Eleanor's dark-eyed gaze looks back at me from a faded photograph. She was beautiful, awkward, complicated. I've read enough to know she adored her father even though he was erratic, that his absence left an ache that shaped her whole life.

Dr. Lawson apparently saw me pick it up. "Eleanor," she says, moving back into the kitchen. "Fascinating woman. Not easy, not sweet, but formidable. Married to a giant shadow, but carried her own light. She adored her father, you know. Even though he was unreliable, troubled. That kind of love doesn't just vanish when someone fails you."

My throat tightens. I press my hand against the page as if I could anchor myself to Eleanor's face.

Dr. Lawson returns with two steaming mugs, sets one in front of me, settles back into her chair with hers. "People forget it's not just policy or speeches that make a leader. It's the wounds they carry. Eleanor's wounds made her. She turned them into strength. But she never stopped longing for her father."

The words hang between us. My chest is heavy. I want to laugh it off, roll my eyes, say something snide about old biographies. Instead I sip the tea, scald my tongue, and sit very still.

Dr. Lawson tilts her head. "You've got that look. Like something you're afraid to name out loud."

I close the book carefully, slide it back into the pile, but my fingers linger on the cover.

"Not today," I whisper.

"Fair enough." She lifts her mug in a mock toast. "History will wait. But so will the truth."

I glance at the book again, then look around the room. Her name is everywhere here—the banners across the quad, the crest on our notebooks, the carved stone above the library doors. Eleanor Roosevelt College.

It strikes me, suddenly, that I've been walking by her name every day since I got here. A woman who carried her wounds into history, who kept longing for a father she couldn't have.

The coincidence makes my chest ache.

I run a finger along the book's spine, then glance around the apartment. Eleanor Roosevelt. The name is stitched on the hoodies, carved in the archways, printed on every official letter I've ever gotten here.

"Can I borrow this?" I ask, holding up the Roosevelt biography.

Her eyebrows shoot up. Then she grins, wide and mischievous. "Of course. Take it. But bring it back, MacKenzie—I know where you live."

I laugh.

She settles onto the arm of her overstuffed chair, her voice dropping into that cadence she uses in lecture halls, the one that makes students forget to look at their phones.

"Eleanor Roosevelt wasn't supposed to be anything. Awkward, too tall, never her mother's favorite. Her father? Brilliant, but troubled. Yet somehow, she carried pieces of him with her. Loyalty. Tenderness. A deep belief in human dignity. She became the conscience of her generation. First Lady, diplomat, human rights crusader. All born from pain she never asked for."

Her words unspool like a story around me, as if the little apartment itself leans closer to listen. I sip the tea and pretend I'm just another student charmed by one of her tangents, but something stirs in my chest, hot and unsettled.

Dr. Lawson leans forward, balancing her tea in one hand, her tone dropping into that hypnotic, storyteller rhythm.

"You know what makes Eleanor so remarkable, Zoe? She came from privilege, sure, but she carried more than her share of loneliness. Her mother thought she was plain, even called her 'Granny' because of her looks. Imagine that. Her father, Elliott Roosevelt—Teddy's younger brother—was handsome, charming, adored her, but he struggled with alcohol and mental illness. He died when she was just a child. She loved him fiercely, but she grew up with the ache of never really having him. And yes— she idolized her Uncle Teddy. Theodore Roosevelt was this larger-than-life figure, a president, a Rough Rider, the American colossus. But Eleanor? She was the shy one, the awkward one. You'd never have picked her as someone destined to change the world."

Dr. Lawson smiles, eyes shining. "But life has a way of roughing us up into who we're meant to be. She married

Franklin, and people dismissed her as his dutiful wife. But after he was struck by polio, she became his legs, his eyes, his ears. And more than that—she found her own voice. She traveled the country, listening to ordinary people. During the Depression, she was sometimes the only one willing to go to the coal camps, the breadlines, the places presidents didn't see. Later, she helped draft the Universal Declaration of Human Rights. That awkward little girl—called 'Granny' by her own mother—helped give the world its conscience."

She pauses, studying Zoe. "History is full of daughters who thought they weren't enough, but turned out to be the only ones who could bear the weight of their own story."

Dr. Lawson takes a sip of tea, then sets the cup down carefully on a stack of books that serve as a side table. Her eyes gleam, the way they always do when she's drawing a thread tight.

Something shifts in my chest, a pressure I've been holding all week. I set the Eleanor Roosevelt biography down on my lap, fingers tracing the embossed spine. My voice, when it comes, is quieter than I intend. "But what if..." I stop, feeling my throat tighten. "What if you don't even know the story you're carrying? What if the people who should've told you....never did?"

She studies me for a long moment. Not rushing. Not rescuing. Just letting the silence hold.

Finally, she says, "Then maybe you start asking the questions they were too afraid to answer."

That lands like a stone dropped into water. I can feel the ripples spreading inside me, dangerous and inevitable. I look down at the book in her lap, at Eleanor's name, and I think of my own. I manage a small smile, closing the book with care. "Thank you, Dr. Lawson."

The professor tilts her head, a little foxlike grin tugging at her mouth. "I'm glad to help. I only hope I did."

"You did," I say, almost too quickly, like if I say it firmly enough it will be true. I rise, clutching the Roosevelt biography in my hands, leaving my cup of tea barely touched on the table.

Dr. Lawson doesn't press, doesn't fuss. She just watches me with that knowing expression she always has, as if she's seen a thousand students at this same precipice before.

I step into the hallway, the door clicking shut behind me. The quiet seems louder than before. I look down at the spine of the book in my hands and whisper, softly enough so no one could hear: "I'll find out."

Chapter Eleven – Hiding Place (Zoe POV)

The rain drives everyone else indoors, lounges crowded, kitchens filled with the smell of popcorn and chatter. I slip across campus with my hood up, clutching the Eleanor biography tight against my chest.

The Castle looms ahead, its turrets slick with drizzle. Students only come here for receptions or piano recitals. For me, it's something else entirely: a sanctuary.

I pad down the picture gallery, past gilt frames of forgotten donors. At the end, the English countryside painting tilts just enough if you know where to press. I push my palm against the side panel. The canvas groans open, revealing a narrow stairwell.

I duck inside, shut the painting, and wait for my eyes to adjust to the darkness. When they do, I move to claim 'my' spot, where there's a very dated floor lamp and chintz armchair that looks like it came from a Vanderbilt child's nursery in the Gilded Age. The glow of the lamp pools over forgotten relics: old costumes still feathered with glitter but covered in dust, cracked leather chairs, cabinets stamped with dates no one remembers.

I curl into the chair with stuffing poking from one arm and open the book. Anna Eleanor Roosevelt was born in 1884…

My throat tightens. What would it have been like to have a father who adored me? Carly's praise always felt conditional, measured out like medicine. Jeff—whatever he is or isn't—remains a shadow I'm not supposed to name.

The lamp hums, daring me to keep reading. I sneeze. That's the only disadvantage in this haven of solitude—the dust. I'm prepared for that too. Ever since I found this spot last semester, I've kept a box of Kleenex and a small bottle of hand sanitizer close by. After blowing my nose, I'm back into the words, reading about Eleanor's childhood loss, her father's death, the grief that shaped her—her resilience. She built herself anyway.

I let the book rest on my lap, staring at the dusty ceiling beams. The rain patters faintly against the stone above. For the first time in weeks I allow myself to sink into the ache of it, here in the quiet, where no one can interrupt or drive it away.

The tiny circle of light cuts across dust motes and broken furniture, keeping the shadows at bay. I pull the lamp closer until the warmth touches my knees, and only then open the biography again.

I sink deeper into the chair, the air heavy with stone and damp. Here in the dark, surrounded by junk and history, I feel anchored for once.

I read of Eleanor's parents—the handsome father who charmed and faltered, the mother whose beauty masked fragility. Eleanor's childhood was punctured by loss, first of her mother, then of her father. My eyes slow on the lines describing his death and the little girl left with a grief that would shape her life.

The words blur together. I lean back into the chair, lamplight spilling across my hands. What I was denied presses in on me now. A father who would have been there, not a ghost glimpsed in fragments, a name spoken like contraband. Carly had painted Jeff (unnamed, of course) as dangerous, reckless, unworthy. But if he was so unworthy, why had Bridget cried when I pressed too hard? Why was she so proud to have known him, collecting his books on her shelves like trophies you only dust but, for some reason, never open? Why did he linger at the edges of everything, never fully gone, never absolutely here?

The lamp hums softly, steady and stubborn, as if daring me to keep reading. I press on, tracing Eleanor's resilience: her admiration for her uncle Teddy, her education, the slow blooming of her voice. I have to build myself up from the fracture, too. My chest rises and falls. I cling to Eleanor's story, as though it might contain a map to navigate my own.

The phone cuts through it. Buzz-buzz-buzz. Vulgar in the quiet. Intent on violating this sacred space.

I glance down. Carly.

For a second I want to let it ring out, but she'll just call again. She always does.

I swipe. "Hi, Mom."

"Where are you?" Sharp. Controlled.

"Studying." True, in its way. I press my thumb against the book's spine, grounding myself.

"With who?"

"By myself."

A pause. I can picture my mother's expression—lips tight, eyes narrowing, as if truth itself was a limited resource that had to be monitored.

"You know, it wouldn't kill you to be more social. Have you been taking your medication?"

"Yes," I hiss. I've been in therapy for anxiety since I was 12.

"You can't afford to start having panic attacks again. And if you need tutoring, ask. Don't... drift."

"I'm fine."

Carly's silence hangs like a verdict. Then: "Good. Don't forget dinner next weekend at the Coopers. I expect you there. It's Ethan's bar mitzvah. It's a big deal."

I lower the phone into my lap, staring at Eleanor's face on the book's cover. The lamp hums on, casting a halo across the page, daring me not to sink.

***

It's next weekend. Baton Rouge smells like wet oak trees and gasoline. I step off the plane and the heat slams me, heavy and wet, like it's trying to pin me in place.

Mom's waiting at baggage claim, smile stretched too wide. Beside her, Bridget waves, Ethan bouncing at her side in a crisp button-down that makes him look older than twelve. I lift my hand, force a smile.

The drive is quiet except for Ethan's chatter in the backseat. He's buzzing, proud, happy. I envy how simple it all seems for him.

The ceremony is first, with Ethan stammering through his Hebrew, his curls tamed with gel, Bridget glowing like she's raising a prophet.

Carly and Bridget smile for the crowd, moving like rival queens forced into the same court. I keep to the edge, letting hugs and handshakes slide past me, retreating and recoiling as much as possible.

After the ceremony, there's a reception at the Coopers' house. The whole world, it feels like, has already gathered. Edward's warm, funny relatives sweep me into hugs that smell like cinnamon and cologne. The house is packed, the air thick with brisket and kugel. Chatter fills the kitchen while trays of food are ushered in and out. Edward beams with paternal pride, Ethan blushes, Bridget moves like a general keeping the machine humming.

Carly floats through the rooms with her polished smile, careful posture, her hand finding the small of my back whenever someone looks our way. Her performance is flawless. Solid as a rock. Controlled, radiating discipline and practiced calm.

I feel like a ghost.

Dinner is worse. The dining room glows with candles and is filled with laughter, Edward telling some joke I don't get, Bridget nodding, Mom chiming in like they've patched every crack between them. They pass bread baskets and salads as if they haven't been circling each other like enemies since last week.

I sit there, pushing couscous around my plate, my chest tightening.

"Eat," Mom whispers beside me, a smile still plastered on. "Don't make this harder."

"I'm not hungry."

Her eyes snap toward me, warning sharp enough to cut.

Bridget notices, of course. She always does. "It's okay, Carly. Big day. She's probably just tired."

But I'm not tired. I'm suffocating.

As Edward proposes a toast, Bridget glows, clutching her son's shoulder, her eyes darting briefly to me—softening for a second before cooling again.

Across the table, Carly raises her glass: "To Ethan. What a beautiful day for such a fine young man."

Her smile doesn't reach her eyes.

Bridget leans in, sweet and sharp. "Yes, and what a blessing we can all be here together. Family is everything, after all."

Their smiles are all teeth.

The words drip like honey, but the undertone is acidic. I see it. Everyone else misses it, or pretends to.

The clink of silverware, Ethan laughing, Edward raising his glass—it all blurs until the words spill out of me, too loud for the table.

"I'm not a Cooper."

The room freezes.

"I don't even know if I'm really a MacKenzie, but I'm not this." I gesture at the table, the candles, the perfect blended family picture. "I don't belong here."

Mom's face drains of color. "Zoe—"

"No." My voice shakes but I don't stop. "I'm done pretending."

Silence swallows the table. Bridget's hand hovers as if she wants to reach for me, but she doesn't. Edward clears his throat, looks at Ethan, then away.

I push back my chair. "Excuse me."

Nobody follows me when I leave.

In the guest room, I grab my bag, still packed from New York because we went straight to the ceremony and then came here afterward. My fingers fumble on my phone as I open the ride-sharing app to reserve a ride back to the airport. Why can't every city have decent transportation like New Yorkers have?

I'm waiting for the ride outside when Carly joins me. "I know you met Jeff. You can't trust him, Zoe."

And I realize then that the very thing she is warning me against—trust—is already shifting. She doesn't trust me —to know what's good for me, to take my medication, to know who my father is.

My father. The key.

By the time headlights sweep the driveway like a pair of watchful eyes, I'm already walking away. I duck my head as I climb in, the cicadas loud in the trees, the air heavy with damp heat.

"Airport?" he asks.

I nod.

By midnight, I'm on a plane back to New York. Layover in Atlanta unfortunately.

Chapter Twelve – Using the Key (Zoe POV)

The flight is a blur. A seatbelt, a crying baby two rows back, the hum of engines like white noise against the storm inside me. I don't wake up until the wheels hit LaGuardia.

I don't text him. I don't call. I don't even let myself think about what I'm doing.

The cab drops me in front of the Shelley on Spring Street and the air is damp and warm, the kind of New York spring that sticks to your skin. I don't text him. I don't call.

This building. His building. I'm standing in front of it, feeling more childish than ever. The last time I was here we entered via the garage, so now I'm seeing for the first time the brass letters above the revolving door, spelling out THE SHELLEY, the kind of lettering I've seen in cemeteries in suburban Atlanta where my grandparents live. Of course I think of Mary Shelley. I read Frankenstein in high school—a life stitched together from secrets, a creation his maker regretted and loved at the same time. Appropriate, I can't help thinking. Because wasn't that me? Jeff must walk under this sign every day. For eighteen years, or however long he's lived here? Everyday. But for me, the word buzzes in my chest like an accusation and a promise: you're not finished. You're becoming.

I shoulder my bag, tug the wheeled suitcase and push my way through the revolving door.

The lobby of the Shelley is cooler—checkered marble underfoot, a faint citrus cleaner in the air. I head for the elevator and only then see it: not just up and down buttons. A keypad.

My throat goes dry.

A woman in sleek leggings and a zip-up steps off the other elevator which has just arrived on the lobby floor. She has a golden retriever tied to her. The woman glances at me, then at the panel.

"You need the code, honey," she says, like we already know each other and she's decided I'm not a problem... yet.

I'm frozen in place at the elevator, stumped by the keypad. I could easily text him and ask for the code, but something stops me from doing that.

"I..." My mouth stumbles. "I'm trying to get to my dad's apartment. He lives here."

Her eyebrows climb. "Who's your dad?"

"Jeff. Jeff Griffin." I swallow. "The writer."

She studies my face like it's a page she's trying to place. At last she sighs and reaches past me, quick fingers on the keys. The elevator chimes and the doors slide open.

"Didn't know he had a family. I can see the resemblance, though." She and the dog are already moving toward the revolving doors that lead outside when she tosses one last look over her shoulder and adds, "Tell him Marcy says hi."

The doors slide shut. I'm alone, breath trapped in my chest as the elevator lurches upward. It groans as it rises, slow and heavy, like it resents being bothered on a weekend. My pulse drums against the small of my throat. I watch my reflection in the steel—braid a little messy, eyes too bright. The numbers blink their slow climb. When the doors open, the hall is as quiet as a church.

I grip the handle of my bag tighter, my other hand pressed to the cool steel wall as if it might steady me. My knees are weak. I force them forward, key in hand.

His loft waits at the end of the hall.

I've come back.

I stop in front of his door. My door? No—don't think that.

The key he gave me feels impossibly small in my palm, as though it can't possibly unlock something as big as this moment. My palm sweats around the key. For a second I think about turning back—calling him, or just not doing this at all. Then I slide the key in. Turn.

I slide it in, twist. A low click, the sound of tumblers yielding. The door gives.

The spell of doubt still lingers as I step inside.

The loft smells faintly of coffee and paper and leather. And pencil, and something sharp—bourbon maybe. And him.

I shut the door behind me, leaning against it, heart racing. The city murmurs through the tall windows.

I'm in. I'm in his world again.

And for the first time in a long time, I feel something close to safe—and something far too dangerous. Something I'm not ready to name yet.

It's empty—the wide space silent but not unfriendly. I step further inside, drop my bag by the door, and breathe.

I don't turn on the lights. I don't move much at all. I just let the hush of his space fold around me, fragile and illicit, like I've stepped into the hollow of his chest.

I wander, zigzagging around the columns and brick partitions. His desk is stacked with drafts. There's an old typewriter there and a MacBook, as if he exists in a portal where time folds inward.

The loft breathes open before me: wide windows pouring light over exposed brick, books stacked in uneven towers. It's messier than I expected. Not dirty—just lived-in. The mess matches me these days. It's so at odds with the neatness and order Carly imposed on my childhood. I like it. It's a breath of fresh air.

The ceiling soars overhead, pipes exposed, morning light spilling through tall factory windows.

The place is both raw and careful—exposed brick, fat old rafters, the big windows that make the city look like a painting. The kitchen sits open in the middle of everything: sink, counters, the stainless steel fridge reflecting it all back.

Shelves lean under the weight of books. There's a stack of messy notes pinned beneath a heavy glass paperweight. On a sideboard: a battered wooden box with little sleeves of stamps inside—tiny portraits of countries, canceled ink like shadows. I touch the edge of the lid and leave it closed.

The silence presses in, enormous, almost holy.

For a moment I just stand in the middle, turning around in place, caught between awe and fear. His world. Safe. Quiet. Messy. I'm here.

And he doesn't even know it yet. I tell myself I'm not snooping. I'm just... seeing. For the first time, I feel the strangeness of belonging nowhere—and yet feeling safe exactly where I am.

Then I see the piano, tucked in a distant corner like a secret he meant to keep from himself, not me. I cross to it before I can talk myself out of it.

The fallboard creaks softly as I slide it back. The keys are cool and a little stubborn, but alive. I sit, tug one foot under me, and let my hands find the shape they always find when I can't fit inside my own chest—Beethoven, the Ninth, the place where everything widens.

The loft catches the sound and turns it into breath. The first phrases steady me. I'm not thinking about Mom or Bridget or the dinner table or the look on Ethan's face when I said I didn't belong. I'm just moving through the river I know.

The lock clicks. The door creaks a little.

I falter, hands hovering, but the door's already swinging open. He steps in— hair damp from the weather, two shopping bags hanging from his fingers like he doesn't know where to put them down.

He stops when he sees me. We stare at each other, the last chord I touched still floating somewhere between us.

"Don't stop," he says, voice low. Not an order. A request.

I look back down the keys. I press down, Moonlight Sonata this time, and the melody takes me again, shakier, but there. From the corner of my eye I see him set the bags beside the door, then come halfway toward me like he's approaching a skittish animal. He sits on the bench without crowding, a careful space between us. I can feel his presence without touching it.

When the last note finally fades, I pull my hands into my lap. My pulse thuds in the quiet.

He exhales like he's been holding his breath the whole time. "I always wanted to learn," he says, a little embarrassed. "Never did."

I nod, not trusting my voice. He stands up and walks over to the bags, fishes around, and produces a ridiculous hardcover book with a shouting cover: *How to Parent Young Adults Without Losing Your Mind*. It's so dumb I bark a laugh before I can stop it. He looks at me, startled, then grins like the sun came out.

"Don't worry," he says. "I'm reading the manual."

He sets the book down and pulls out something else—a matte-black helmet. He turns it in his hands, the visor catching the light. "This is for you. If you're ever on the bike with me." He hesitates. "Only if you want to be."

I run my thumbnail along the piano's fallboard, sliding it over the keys, then glance at the helmet. "I look terrible in helmets," I say, which is not a no.

"Me too," he says. "It builds character."

The line is so stupid it works. Some of the tightness in my throat loosens. The whole room hums like it remembers the notes better than I do.

He doesn't push. He just stands there, as if the only thing he's trying to prove is that he'll stay put if I need him to.

Amazing myself, I believe him.

Chapter Thirteen – Waking Up in His World (Zoe POV)

I wake up to sunlight pouring through the window in rays that cut across the bed, cut up by the shadows cast by the window pattern. Not the filtered, swampy sun of Louisiana slipping through blinds, but a hard, golden New York light pouring over a skyline. For a moment, I don't know where I am. The bed is too big, the sheets smell like soap and him, and the ceiling stretches so high above me it feels like I've been lifted into some cathedral.

And then I remember: the loft. Jeff.

I sit up slowly. His bed, my bed for now. He's on the futon upstairs, in the loft. I hear him turn over once, then silence.

Bare feet on cold wood. I pad to the window, push aside the curtain — rooftops, water towers, the jagged teeth of buildings. Nothing in Louisiana looked like this. I feel dizzy, like I've landed on another planet. I barely know him, I barely know this place, but I feel safe, and I'm beginning to trust him. I don't know why. I've never felt this before. I just know it's better than anything I've ever known.

In the kitchen, the memory of the only other time I woke up here helps me find the coffee. His system is almost too neat — mugs lined like soldiers, silverware exactly even. I put water on, figure out the French press, clumsy but determined. It feels like a little rebellion: claiming space here, daring to use his things.

The smell wakes him. He stirs, groans, and sits up, hair wild. Glasses on his eyes (too early for contacts) which go straight to the empty bed. I watch the panic flood his face until he sees me standing at the counter. He exhales so loudly it makes me laugh into my mug.

"You move like a ghost," he says, voice gravelly.

"I made coffee. Hope I didn't break your system."

"You broke nothing," he says, standing and stretching, still half-dreaming. He points at the piano in the corner. "Though that thing hasn't woken up in years."

I glance at it, then back to him. "Maybe it was waiting for me."

He doesn't answer — just looks at me with something too deep to read.

We sit, me with coffee, him with nothing yet. Silence, but not hostile. A silence filled with language. His eyes move toward the record player, then to the bookshelf, then back to me, as if he's offering me keys without words: pick one. Music, story, or both.

I don't take the bait. Not yet. Instead I raise my mug. "Thanks for letting me stay."

He nods, then gets up, rummages in a drawer. When he turns back, he's holding a box of mix, a waffle iron, and a grin.

"I made waffles for you last time," he says. "They're just as good in the morning as the afternoon."

And just like that, the morning tilts. A secret life building itself out of ordinary things.

While he mixes the batter, I set my empty mug down and wander back toward the piano. The score book is thick, frayed at the edges, smelling faintly of dust. Chopin, Debussy, Rachmaninoff—all the ghosts waiting for hands. My fingers hover, itching to play something fierce, something that would burn the morning air clean. But I can't. Not with my phone buzzing, buzzing, buzzing in the bag by the bed.

I slam the score book shut, dust flying. "She always does this. Tightens the leash, turns everything into a crisis. I can't breathe around her. I just—" I stop, because my voice is shaking and I hate that.

I feel his hands on my shoulders. It stuns me, but I don't move. Instead, I lean in, allowing him to steady me. He gently pulls me backward into him, wrapping his arms around me. He doesn't kiss me or do anything else but hold me with his arms. At last the phone stops its ceaseless buzzing.

"I know it's Carly. She knows I came back. I don't know why she has to do this."

"Zoe, I would do the same. If you boarded a flight somewhere, I'd check in, make sure you got there safely." His voice is steady, annoyingly calm. "Making your mother worry isn't going to do anything good. Go call her.""

"You don't know what she's like," I say in a childish tone that sounds foreign.

"Maybe not, but all you have to do is tell her the truth, that you're here and you're safe. That you need space. That you want to stay here."

 It sounds so easy when he says it. Like breathing. Like music. But my throat feels raw.

"What if she says I shouldn't be here?" I spin around and look at him. "Because she will, Jeff. She'll say I shouldn't trust you, that I should stay away from you."

He flinches and for a second he looks like I punched him. I want him to say it: You're right, your mom's crazy, I'll protect you. I want it so badly it hurts.

He recovers. Grins. "Then you tell her if you feel like leaving, you'll go back to school, but not until he makes you waffles."

I smile back in spite of myself. "Fine," I whisper. Not because I'm brave but because I'm tired of running.

I slip away to find my bag that holds the cursed anti-privacy device.

As he returns to the batter, he says, "You'll feel better once it's out of the dark. Then you and I will have the rest of the day to ourselves. Just us."

Something lifts in me, light as air. It feels like the start of a pact, fragile but real: face the storm, then find our own quiet after.

The phone feels heavy in my hand. My thumb hovers over her name. I imagine Carly's face when she sees it's me—tight with fury, but lit with relief. I press call.

She answers on the first ring.

"Zoe. Where are you? You better be at the dorm."

"I'm fine." My voice comes out steadier than I feel. "I'm in SoHo."

"In So—" Her words splinter into static anger. "You're with him, aren't you? He put you up to this."

"No. Mom, this was me. I need space. I'm not a child anymore."

There's silence, brittle as glass. Then: "You think living with him is better? He hasn't been there for you once in your life."

I squeeze the phone so hard my knuckles ache. "You're wrong. He's here now. And I want to be here too."

"You're throwing everything away," she hisses. "Your future, your stability—"

"I'm not throwing it away. I'm finding it." My voice cracks, but I don't back down. "You've never heard me, Mom. Not about Dad, not about me. I'm not saying I hate you, I just... I can't breathe in your house. I need something else."

For a long beat, only her breath comes through, ragged, wounded. Then softer, almost inaudible: "Zoe..."

I swallow the ache in my throat. "I'll call you. I promise. But I'm staying here."

Before she can reel me back in, I hang up. My hand shakes as I let the phone drop on the bed.

Jeff has stayed by the sink the whole time, silent. When I glance at him, his face is unreadable. Then he nods once. "Good. That's done."

Just like that, the mood shifts. The anxiety doesn't vanish, but it moves off my chest, leaves me room to breathe.

For the second time, Jeff makes us the best waffles I've ever tasted in my life. Only this time they're better. I'm better.

I help him load the dishwasher, his sleeves rolled up, deliberate in every movement like he's been living alone too long and ritual has replaced conversation.

The Laugh (Jeff POV)

I'm rinsing glasses in the kitchen when I catch Zoe's side of a phone call, her voice carrying over from where she's sitting on the bed. What hits me more than anything are the words, "You've never heard me, Mom. Not about me. Not about Dad." It's not just that Zoe called me Dad in that spontaneous moment (although that feels amazing.) It's more the hint of Carly that comes through in the sentence. It's almost two decades since I was face to face with the woman, but I remember the careful mask she wore, the discipline and control that guided her every move, like it was yesterday. That's the thing about Carly that has kept me at bay, long before that night, and certainly after it. Before that night, there were glimpses behind the mask only when she laughed, and now when I hear Zoe laugh, it's like I'm hearing Carly again. It's the laugh I remember. It's that laugh that has haunted me for all this time.

Spending Time Together (Zoe POV)

We leave the Shelley together. He insists on walking, his long stride careful to match mine. SoHo turns into Greenwich Village. He takes me to the little independent bookstores tucked on side streets—rows of creaking shelves, cats perched on counters, handwritten staff picks. He doesn't hover but he watches me, a quiet pride in his eyes every time I stop to read a spine.

At lunch, we sit in a tiny café with mismatched chairs, sunlight spilling across our plates. I order a grilled cheese, he gets black coffee and something he barely touches. I think about Carly's voice, sharp in my ear, and then look at him across the table. His silence isn't judgment, it's space.

***

In the afternoon, we meet his friends Theo and Julia in Central Park. Theo makes a production out of it, waving both arms from a blanket near the pond, cracking jokes with sign language. His hands move faster than his grin, fingers flying through the air.

[About time. I thought you ditched me for chess with the old men.]

Jeff signs back, slower, deliberate. [Traffic.]

[Spare us the excuses,] Theo signs back.

Julia is warm, her laugh like bells, her eyes sharp as if she already knows my story. "They're already bickering in stereo," she says to me, passing me a cold bottle of water.

Theo springs up and folds me into a hug. He pulls back, eyes bright, and signs directly to me: [I'm Theo. You must be Zoe. Finally.]

I blink, startled—and then answer. [Yes. Nice to meet you.] My hands flow without hesitation, muscle memory from camp three summers ago, the last summer Carly made me go.

Theo's eyebrows jump. [You sign?!]

[A little,] I say, signing along, cheeks warm. [I learned at camp.]

Theo shoots Jeff a look. [You didn't tell me she knew.]

Jeff shrugs, sheepish, but I can see the pride sneaking onto his face.

We all drop onto the blanket. Julia digs into a canvas tote and pulls out cones. "Vanilla with sprinkles," she says, handing one to me. "Theo insisted. He swore he could tell."

I laugh. "He was right."

Theo watches us, then signs with mock suspicion. [You eat ice cream? You pass the test.]

The group falls into rhythm, with Theo signing with machine-gun energy, Julia translating when Jeff doesn't keep up, Jeff jumping in with corrections that make Theo roll his eyes. I keep signing along, surprised at how quickly it comes back.

At one point Theo leans across and signs privately to me, sharp and mischievous: [He's nervous. Don't let him fool you.]

I glance at Jeff. He's busy trying to retell one of Theo's stories verbally for Julia's benefit. He looks so at ease and yet... not. He doesn't laugh as much as the rest of us, but he watches. And I can feel it, as steady as the summer sun: he's proud of me.

I sign back to Theo. [So am I.]

Theo grins like he's known me all my life.

And for the rest of the afternoon, while the sun flickers through the trees and New Yorkers drift by, I feel like I've been let into a circle that was always meant to include me.

Trust (Jeff POV)

The four of us squeeze into a car on the E train out to Forest Hills, pressed between a saxophonist warming up at the far end and a pair of tourists arguing over the map. Zoe sits beside me, her tote balanced on her knees, the Eleanor Roosevelt biography peeking out.

Across from us, Theo signs something crude about the saxophonist. Julia smacks his arm without even needing to look, already knowing what he said.

I can't help but laugh, my hands moving without thought. [You're just mad you never learned an instrument.]

Theo shoots back instantly. [You sing Bob Dylan off-key, that counts as an instrument?]

I think with pride about Zoe playing the piano, but I decide to keep the banter going. [Careful, buddy,] I warn him. [If Blackthorn does make a comeback, he might show up in Forest Hills again.] This is a long-running joke between myself and my friends, who hold a half-serious grudge against me to this day for writing *A Body in Forest Hills*, the fourth book in the Blackthorn series.

Julia rolls her eyes mockingly as she translates out loud for Zoe and adds, "Please keep your morose detective out of our backyard."

Zoe is watching me instead of them, however, her brow furrowed in something between curiosity and awe.

"You're really good," she says quietly. "Like… fluent."

I shrug. "Had to be," I say, signing the words at the same time, letting her watch the words instead of just hearing them. [Theo didn't have many people willing to learn. I didn't have many people willing to stay.]

Theo sees it, his smile softening into something quieter. He signs toward Zoe, [He never left me. Not once.]

Zoe catches it—her eyes widen, lips parting, almost whispering the English. "Not once."

The train rattles on, screeching through the tunnel. Julia starts telling a story about Theo at the DMV, and everyone laughs. But Zoe keeps looking at my hands, like the movement itself has given her another key to me.

She finally asks, "Will you teach me more?"

I nod. "Yeah. Anytime."

And for the rest of the ride, with the city rushing by in blurs of light and shadow, she mirrors me: fingers clumsy but determined, forming the signs for [father], [daughter], [safe.] My heart heavy, I recall her referring to me as "Dad" on the phone with Carly that morning. *You've never heard me, Mom. Not about Dad, not about me. I'm not saying I hate you, I just... I can't breathe in your house. I need something else.*

Dad. The appellation makes my mouth go dry. I guess all the water has gone to my eyes. I wonder if she even caught it or was it an unconscious slip of the tongue? If the latter, how much more amazing that she would call me Dad or Father without thinking about it. It means that she is feeling it before her mind has a chance to intervene. She trusted me this morning when I wrapped my arms around her and advised her to call Carly.

There's something going on between them. I know so little about parenting, I hardly trust myself to know how to deal with it. I know the first step is to understand it and the only way to get there is to gain Zoe's trust completely, by showing her I'm here, and that I'm not going anywhere.

Noir Fans (Zoe POV)

The E train rattled, brakes screeching at Roosevelt Avenue. While my dad and his friends joked about one of his books, I looked around the train. Two seats down, a man tipped back his book to check the station sign, and the glossy back cover angled right toward me.

Bold text leapt out in the flicker of the fluorescent lights: "Riveting! Griffin has given us another page turner from Detective Blackthorn, not in the Crescent City for a change, but right in the boroughs of our city!" — The New Yorker.

My throat tightened. The man lowered the book, oblivious. It was the very title Theo had mentioned: A Body in Forest Hills, being read, apparently, by a random Queens commuter, to whom it must have been just another subway distraction. To me it was a flare, reminding me that my dad's name, my dad's stories, belonged everywhere—in glossy reviews, in strangers' hands—before I'd ever been allowed to claim him.

I turned my face to the scratched window, pretending to watch the tunnel. One sentence. One stranger. And suddenly it felt like I was in line behind a thousand people who'd gotten to know him first.

Theo's House (Jeff POV)

When we step into the Arceneaux living room, Zoe's eyes go straight to the books, then the photographs on the mantel. I watch her eyes land on one in particular—the wedding shot, me in a tux next to Theo, both of us younger but solid, anchored.

Her gaze shifts when Julia lowers herself onto the sofa, one hand pressed to the curve of her belly. It shows more than just a couple of weeks ago when I came for dinner. She's solidly in the second trimester now. Julia flinches, grabbing her belly with both hands.

Zoe freezes. I catch the flicker of surprise that breaks through her careful mask.

Julia notices and smiles. "She's making herself known these days."

Theo signs something quick, his expression mischievous. Julia laughs before translating. "He says Jeff's been pestering us about names. Like it's his kid."

Heat rises in my face. I wave it off, but I can feel Zoe's eyes lingering on me. The realization is quiet, unspoken, but it hangs between us: I never left them. I've been here all these years, through milestones, while she grew up believing I didn't care about her.

Julia smooths her blouse over the swell of her belly. Theo rests his hand protectively on her knee. I sink into an armchair across from them, too familiar with this room, too at home. Zoe takes it all in—the comfort, the history —and I see Carly's impression unraveling in her eyes.

"Any progress on names yet?" I ask, trying to shift the weight.

Julia sighs, smiling. "We've narrowed it down."

Theo signs something brisk. [Don't tell him yet.]

Julia rolls her eyes.

"Come on," I tease, leaning forward to catch Theo's hands. "It's Jeff, right? Nice, simple, timeless."

Zoe blinks, startled. "But it's a girl."

"That's the beauty of it," I grin at her. "Trailblazing. First of her kind. Imagine it—Jeff, Queen of the Kindergarten."

Julia covers her face, laughing so hard she nearly spills her sparkling water. Theo signs an exaggerated scold, and the room ripples with warmth. Even Zoe's lips twitch, like she's fighting not to laugh. I feel the faint weight of trust begin to settle. She's still fighting Carly's poison against me, but it grows weaker by the minute.

She drifts back toward the mantel, drawn to the photographs. Her hand hovers over the frame. "You were the best man?"

I shrug, but Theo's already signing, his eyes gleaming.

Julia smirks. "Oh, you should hear this."

"Please don't," I groan.

Theo's hands move faster. Julia bursts out laughing.

I mutter the translation, blemishing my reputation in front of my own daughter. "I dropped the rings. Right in the middle of the vows. Whole church went silent while they rolled down the aisle."

Julia wipes her eyes, gasping with laughter. "His face was the color of a beet."

Zoe's grin is reluctant but real. "Seriously?"

Theo signs again, and I translate, resigned. "He says he's lucky the priest didn't call the whole thing off."

The laughter settles, warm as an old quilt. And then Theo signs something slower, his face gentle.

Doubt (Zoe POV)

I laugh too, surprised at how natural it feels. This isn't the Jeff I knew—the man who showed up suddenly and tore open the ground under me. This is someone different: teased, belonging, tethered.

Another signed exchange, slower this time, Theo's eyes fix on Jeff. My father's voice softens as he translates. "He says... he doesn't have a brother by blood. But I'm it. And now you're here, too."

Something cracks open in my chest. I blink fast and turn back to the mantel before anyone notices, staring too hard at Julia's bouquet in the wedding photo.

But the question pushes up anyway, undeniable. My voice sounds small when I ask it, but steady: "Then why... why weren't you there for me?"

Understanding (Jeff POV)

Her words hit like a blade sliding between my ribs. Not shouted, not even angry—just steady, bare. That makes it worse. A quiet knife, slicing all the air out of the room, the question I've dreaded all along.

My mouth opens but nothing comes out. My chest tightens, years of silence pressing into a knot that refuses to loosen.

Why wasn't I there? I could list the facts: Carly never told me, I never checked in. I sealed myself off even from Facebook interactions. I could say I was young, reckless, broke, too full of myself. I could blame the world. But none of it feels enough, not when her eyes pin me now, searching for something true.

I swallow hard. Other fathers' excuses—about court battles, restraining orders, custody fights—aren't there to shield me. Because the truth is worse in its way.

"I didn't know," I say, and even to my own ears it sounds thin, pathetic. "Zoe… I swear to you, I didn't know you existed. Not until that day in the bookstore."

Her eyes narrow, sharp, cutting, years written in the flicker of her face. I push on, fumbling, desperate for her to hear me.

"Carly told you I left, didn't she? That I… chose not to be there."

A flicker gives me the answer.

"That's not true," I say quickly, leaning forward. "She never told me. She never gave me the chance. Carly—" I stop, force the anger back down. No good will come of turning this into a Carly-bashing match.

The silence thickens. Julia shifts. Theo signs something, his face taut with sympathy.

I rake my hand through my hair. "What I'm guilty of— what I'll carry—is not staying closer to Bridget. Not checking in. Not keeping that line open. If I had, I'd have known. I should've known. That's on me."

The admission burns because it's true—I let time, pride, stubborn distance harden into silence. And in that silence, Zoe grew up without me.

"I can't fix the years," I say softly. "And I can't take back what you missed. But I need you to believe me when I say: if I had known about you, nothing would've kept me away. Nothing."

Her gaze stays steady, unreadable. I brace for rejection, for her to turn cold, to walk. But beneath the fear there's something else—a trembling, fragile hope I haven't let myself feel in eighteen years.

Clarity (Zoe POV)

"I didn't know."

The words land and just sit there, heavy, foreign, like a sentence in a language I should've known but didn't.

I want to laugh, scream, call him a liar. Too easy—of course he'd say that. What man wouldn't? But the way he says it, like it hurts him more than me, catches in my chest.

"You didn't know," I repeat, testing it, rolling it around in my mouth as if saying it might make it feel less impossible.

My whole life has been built on Carly's version: the boyfriend in Atlanta, the one who didn't want me. The empty space that was supposedly him. Mom's bitterness whenever I asked too much. She always seemed so certain. So righteous.

And yet here he is—my father—looking at me with eyes that don't flinch, don't dart away, don't try to dress the truth in something prettier. He says it like a confession, not an excuse.

I cross my arms tight against me. "She told me you left. She told me… you didn't want me." My voice cracks, sharper than I mean, and I hate that.

He leans forward, voice low, steady. "That's not true. If I'd known, nothing would've kept me away."

I search him, hard as I can, like I'll find the lie written across his forehead. All I see is guilt—real, raw—and something else. Something terrifying. Hope.

It terrifies me because it sparks the same thing in me. A hope I don't want, a hope that could wreck me if it isn't true.

I want to run. I want to scream. I want, for one second, to believe him. And that's the scariest part.

The words spill out, hot and shaky: "When I went to that signing in Bronxville…" My throat tightens, but I force myself to look at him. "I wasn't just there by accident. I knew Bridget had this old boyfriend. The famous writer." My laugh is bitter, small. "She used to drop your name like trivia—and I'd file it away. And somewhere in my head I made this… story. That maybe—just maybe—you were the one. My dad."

The words feel like glass in my throat, every shard sharper than the last. "I didn't know about you and Carly.

Not then. She always said it was someone else. Atlanta guy, the one who wanted nothing to do with me. That was the story. That was all I had."

He sits so still I think he hasn't breathed since I began. Then he leans forward, voice breaking at the edges: "Zoe—if I had known… wild horses couldn't have kept me away from you. Not for a day. Not for a year. Certainly not for eighteen."

Something splits wide inside me. All those years of wondering, of inventing, of pretending not to care while secretly craving the answer—I wasn't crazy. I hadn't made it up. The fantasy I clung to in secret, the dream I was almost ashamed of, is standing right here telling me it could have been real.

And now it is.

My breath goes ragged, chest seizing, and I fold in on myself like my body can't take its own weight.

He's out of his chair before I even realize I'm falling, kneeling in front of me, careful, so careful, like I'm made of glass. "Zoe. Hey. I've got you."

That's all it takes. The sobs rip through me, violent and humiliating, years of silence and swallowing questions finally tearing their way out. My hands shake as I try to cover my face, hide the mess of myself, but he just lays a hand lightly on my wrist—not pulling, not prying—just there.

"I'm sorry," I gasp through it, though I don't even know who I'm apologizing to. To him, for the years we lost? To myself, for wanting so much? To Carly, even, for betraying her version of the story?

"Don't be sorry." His voice is low, husky with something that might be his own tears. "Don't ever be sorry for this."

I finally let my forehead fall against his shoulder, shaking and burning and utterly undone, and he doesn't flinch. He doesn't retreat. He holds steady, letting me pour it all out.

We stay like that until my breathing slows, until the storm spends itself and I can lift my head again. His shirt is wet where my face had been, and I almost laugh through the wreck of myself.

"You've got me now," he says, simple as that. And for the first time, I believe it.

Connection (Jeff POV)

The subway rocks and rattles beneath us. Zoe sits across from me, her knees pulled in, her braid slipping over her shoulder. She's quiet, calmer than earlier, but still watchful, guarded.

An older woman across the aisle squints at me, then digs into her tote. She pulls out a battered copy of my latest novel and holds it up like proof.

"You're Jeff Griffin, aren't you?" she asks.

I nod, and she beams, passing me a pen. I sign the title page while the car sways, hand the book back, and she thanks me like I've given her gold.

When I glance up, Zoe's watching, her mouth curled in a half-smile. She raises her hands and signs — quick, a little sloppy, but clear enough: [Big shot.]

I can't help but laugh. I sign back, [Not impressed?]

She rolls her eyes, and for a moment, the tension between us eases into something light.

At the next stop, we climb the stairs to the street. The evening air smells like fried garlic and hot asphalt. She checks her phone, and I ask what she's in the mood for.

"Dumplings," she says, almost immediately.

We order from a hole-in-the-wall place near the station and carry the cartons back toward Spring Street. Zoe walks half a step ahead of me, swinging the bag of takeout, and for the first time all day, I let myself believe we might find a rhythm.

Back at the Shelley, the city lights bleed in through the high windows. She disappears into the shower, leaving a trail of steam and the faint smell of her shampoo. I set out the cartons on the counter, crack open a bottle of sparkling water, and wait for her to come back—wondering how long this fragile truce will last.

Chapter Fifteen – Making Room for Her

Neighbors (Jeff POV)

The week slips by in its own quiet rhythm. I spend more time at the Shelley than usual, waiting on deliveries. When the team from the furniture store finally shows up, I guide them through the lobby and into the elevator, keeping an eye on the bed frame and the boxes stacked around it. I hold the doors open for the delivery crew, two guys in gray shirts maneuvering a boxed bed frame. Behind them comes a nightstand, a desk, the whole set I picked out for Zoe earlier in the week. New furniture for the upstairs nook. Her space. The loft within the loft.

We wheel everything across the tiles just as the other elevator dings. Marcy steps out, tugging along her golden retriever. The dog sniffs at the boxes and wags his tail like we've brought him a treat. Marcy lives three floors down, a relentless runner with that impeccably trained retriever always at her side. We nearly collide.

"Jeff," she says with that neighborly half-smile. "Looks like you're finally settling down."

"Something like that," I mutter, steadying the bed frame before it clips the wall.

Her smile sharpens. "I met your daughter."

I freeze, hand still on the elevator door.

"She was here a few weeks ago," she goes on. "Trying to figure out the keypad. Sweet girl. A little lost. Said you were her dad."

The words knock something loose inside me. "Zoe."

"Zoe," she repeats, tasting the name. "She looks like you. Eyes. Jaw. No mistaking that one." Then her voice softens. "She's welcome company. This building could use a little youth. She was so sweet, asking me for help with the code. Just don't let her grow up too fast here. New York has a way of doing that."

I don't know what to do with my hands, so I shove them in my pockets. The delivery guy mutters about getting this show on the road.

I nod, throat tight. "I'll keep that in mind."

The elevator doors slide closed between us. "Top floor," I tell the movers, my voice rougher than I mean it to be.

Zoe fumbling with the keypad, admitting she needed help. Innocent, like she hasn't yet built up the armor this city demands. That scares the hell out of me. Because innocence means she's still a kid—breakable, trusting. But the thought of her "growing up" carries its own kind of terror. If she sheds that softness, if she hardens into some cynical professional, I'll mourn that too.

The cruel paradox: I want her to stay a girl forever and I want her to grow up safe and strong. Both at once. Contradictions baked into fatherhood.

Don't grow up. But don't stay naïve.

A father can't win.

I shove the thought aside, guiding the crew into the open elevator. Still, it rides with me all the way up.

Visibility (Zoe POV)

Friday, the train hums beneath me, rocking steady as it pulls out of Bronxville. I've got my earbuds in, trying to memorize Schubert's Impromptus so I can play them on Jeff's piano—my piano, he insists.

"No, it's yours," he told me last week when I said I was going to play his piano. "If you keep calling it mine, I'm going to spray paint your name on it."

I knew he was teasing, but it felt good. He teases more and more now. At first, it felt weird, but then I started liking it, and now I expect it. I want to play something for him besides Beethoven. Yes, the Ninth Symphony and Moonlight Sonata are my favorites, but he seems so content and peaceful when I play them, I want to see what else I can dazzle him with. I guess I just want that feeling—his pride washing over me—as much as I can elicit.

Owen's voice replays in my head. I barely know the guy but he stopped me on the quad before I caught the train. The way he grinned when he called out, "Hey, MacKenzie —don't forget to apply for the Herald in the fall. Sophomore staffers can start in September."

MacKenzie. He always says it like he's trying it on, crisp, deliberate, like he likes the sound.

I stammered something about maybe, and he shrugged, easy, confident. Then he tilted his head. "So how'd it go? Your interview with Griffin?"

I blinked, completely thrown. "What interview?"

"The one he came back for, to do with you. He said he wanted to answer your questions, but I guess you disappeared. He said he wanted to find you if he could. I told him you might be in the library since you work there."

I laughed it off, moving along before he could see how weird it landed. But the word interview stuck. Jeff must've made it up as a pretext for looking for me. Jeff playing detective, like Blackthorn in his novels, on a mission to stalk his daughter. Cute. I'll definitely be teasing him about that.

But what's this about Owen thinking I actually interviewed Jeff Griffin? My father. I know Owen has no idea Jeff is my dad, but still. Does he really expect me to write about him for the paper? Some kind of audition? A test?

The train carries me south toward the city. I turn it over like a stone in my pocket. Owen, with his sharp green eyes and editor's notebook sticking out of his jacket, thought Jeff Griffin—my father—talked to me for an article. Which meant Jeff had been on campus under false pretenses. Which meant Owen had met him. Which meant Owen… somehow ties me with Jeff.

That Owen even knows me at all is incredible. I spoke to him once last semester, my first, just to ask about joining the Herald. He shut me down—no freshmen.

I press my forehead to the glass, hiding behind my reflection. Does Owen… like me? He teased me once, back in the fall, about showing up at an open mic with a notebook full of half-finished poems. I wanted to disappear, but then he asked if I was still thinking about the paper.

Boys never looked at me twice in high school. I wasn't the girl with glossy hair and easy jokes. I was the one with panic pills in her bag and a stack of books heavier than her backpack could take. A late bloomer, Bridget always said, like it was inevitable.

But Owen… he noticed me. Twice. And that makes me restless.

The announcement for Grand Central pulls me out of my thoughts. I shove my phone in my pocket, pulse quickening as the train slows. Owen fades for the moment, replaced by the reality of where I'm headed: the Shelley. The weekend. My father.

Still, as I step onto the platform, the question clings like heat in the tunnels: does Owen actually like me? And what will I even do if he does?

Writing Again (Jeff POV)

<u>Working Titles</u>

Sound of Silence: Stories for My Daughter

Proof and Sound: Breaking the Silence

(I don't know yet which is right. Maybe neither. Maybe the act of writing will tell me. One feels like a whisper to you alone, the other like something someone might shelve in a bookstore. You'll see both here, because I'm not ready to decide what this is. Maybe you'll be the one to choose.)

I should probably start with the lie.

The lie was that I was always meant to be a writer. That I had some grand design, that there was destiny in it. That's what they'll print in profiles, the neat version: Jeff Griffin, crime novelist, New York Times bestseller, destined for the page from day one.

That's bullshit.

The truth is I wrote because I had nothing else. Because I was stubborn. Because I hated myself too much to quit but not enough to believe I could be great.

I wanted to be a playwright once. Big mistake. A play isn't just words on a page — it's begging people to show up, to clap, to tell you that you matter. When they didn't, I

learned quick: failure doesn't come with violins. It comes
with empty seats.

So I pivoted. Crime sells, I told myself. People want blood.
People want bodies in alleys, bad men with guns. It
wasn't art, but it was a paycheck. And I needed a
paycheck, because the alternative was more dish pits,
more copyediting, more temp gigs where they look
through you like you're invisible.

But the real failure—the only one that still keeps me
awake—isn't a play or a novel or a review. It's that there's
a 18-year-old girl out there who had to find me on her
own. Because I wasn't there. Because I didn't know.
Because maybe, deep down, I didn't want to know.

That's the ugly part. That's the marrow of it.

I'll tell it all, if I can stand it.

***

By Friday afternoon, the room upstairs is transformed:
bed, dresser, nightstand, desk, lamp, chair—all waiting
for her. A little apartment inside mine. I tuck clean sheets
on the bed, but stop at the fitted one, thinking she'll want
to finish the rest herself. They're her things. Her room.
She should make it her own.

That evening, Zoe comes in, hair mussed from the
subway, her crossbody bag slung low. Her eyes flick
toward the stair-ladder, registering the change.

"You didn't waste time," she says, brushing past me—half
teasing, half reverent.

"Welcome home," I tell her.

I've stopped at a deli on the way back—containers of food that only need reheating. We'll heat them later, but for now I set the bag on the counter. She drops onto one of the stools with a sigh.

"Finals in two weeks. I'm already dying." She props her chin in her hand. "Dr. Lawson assigns practically a book a week. Six total for World Civ. And that's just one class. Biology's a nightmare, and my Writing and Research paper—don't even ask. I picked the death penalty. What was I thinking?"

Her laugh is small, brittle.

"Ah, yes. Finals. All-nighters, caffeine. I remember. How's that going?"

"Oh, you know." She waves a hand. "Just drowning, no big deal." Then her eyes narrow at me. "And you?"

I take a breath. "Writing again."

"Writing what?"

The word catches, but I force it out. "Memoir." It sounds heavier than I want, and I glance at her like I'm asking permission.

She leans forward, cautious but curious. "Memoir?"

"Yeah."

"It's... your whole life?" she whispers. "I mean, I saw your Wikipedia page, but it doesn't really say much."

"Warts and all," I admit. "Not just the bullet points—everything. The truth."

She repeats the word under her breath, testing it. "The dirty laundry."

I let it hang, then pivot. "Come here. I want to show you something."

I lead her over to my desk in the corner. On top sits the old typewriter I tracked down on eBay—clunky, scuffed, faintly smelling of machine oil. A Woodstock, 1920. Still works like a dream. I slide in a sheet of paper and punch a few keys just to hear the click.

Her head tilts. "Neat. Are you going to type your memoir on it?"

"You're kidding, right? Of course. It makes me feel closer to Hemingway. Tennessee Williams. More worthy to call myself a writer."

"When did you know you were going to be a writer?" she asks suddenly.

"Whew," I whistle. "That's a hell of a question. I guess when I realized I was too stubborn to quit."

She smirks. "So that's it?"

"What's what?"

"How you know what you want to do. It's the thing you just do… because you have to. Like Eleanor Roosevelt and social justice."

I grin crookedly. "Still reading the Eleanor Roosevelt book?"

"I finished it. I returned it to its owner."

"And who's that?"

"Dr. Lawson."

"Ah, the World Civ professor. I'd like to meet her."

"She'd like to meet you too. I told her about you."

That pulls me up short. "Oh?" Zoe talking about me at college.

"She's the only one I talk to."

I frown. "Ever?" I realize I've never heard her mention friends her own age.

She shrugs. "She's a good listener. She's always there. Lives in an apartment on the ground floor of the dorm. Open door policy."

"Huh. Peculiar. A teacher living in a freshmen dorm." My gut twinges—something to worry about?

"Oh, yeah. She's very peculiar. That's what I like about her."

"What do you like about her? Actually—hold that thought. Let's talk over food. I'm starving."

Talking (Zoe POV)

While he scoops spinach lasagna, buttered brussels sprouts, and bread rolls onto plates for reheating, I tell him about Dr. Lawson. I can see him visibly relaxing about her as I explain what a relief it is to meet someone who is never fake or pushy, but always direct and honest. At the same time, her honesty is not unkindness. "She just sees. Really sees. Like no one else."

"And this is Zoe MacKenzie's friend at Roosevelt College, the one who sees."

"Are you making fun of me?"

"Never," he says earnestly, making eye contact. "I just think it's interesting that, of all the people you mention, of all the people to befriend at Roosevelt College, it's the tenured professor who lives in the dorm, the twice divorced, hoarder of books, with an open door, inviting students to come sit with her anytime. Not your suite mates, or anyone you work with at the library."

"Well, my suite mates are just random people I was assigned to."

He nods. "I get it."

"Do you?"

"Umhmm. You're like me. You're drawn to solitude and when it comes to friendship you won't accept anything less than the pure of heart."

"Like Theo?"

He takes a sip of ice water. "Yep."

This similarity between us hangs in the air until he adds, "But, Zoe, Theo and I are the same age. We became friends in third grade."

"OK, I see what you mean, but it's not like I don't talk to people my age. Why, just today, before I got on the train, I had a little chat with Owen. You met Owen."

He looks at me questioningly, as if the name is not ringing any bells.

"Owen Aubrey, editor of the Roosevelt Herald."

Recognition. "Ah, yes. Sorry.

"He wants me to interview you."

He laughs. "What?"

"Well, apparently, you told him you went up there to find me because I had questions, but I disappeared. He expects my first article for the paper, once I'm officially a sophomore, to be an article about you."

He puts his fork down and stares at me.

I don't know what to say. Interview me? Her? Why is she telling me this now? I can't help wondering if it's just a deflection. On the other hand, if her future boss is really expecting her to interview me….

"Did he actually use that word—interview?" I ask, trying to keep my voice even.

She nods, watching me closely, like she's testing how much I'll squirm.

I lean back in my chair, fork abandoned on the plate. "That's a hell of a way to start a journalism career—writing about your old man." I give a crooked smile, but inside the thought is twisting my guts. What the hell did I tell Owen, exactly? I'd been improvising that day, desperate to find her, and now the lie is circling back.

Her eyes are steady, unblinking. "Would you let me?"

I almost laugh. Let her? She could drag every skeleton out of my closet if she wanted to. But it's the way she asks it—tentative, almost hopeful—that knocks me sideways.

"I don't know if I'm the right subject for you, Zo," I say slowly. "I've spent years trying to keep people out of my head. And you… you'd be walking straight in."

She tilts her head, braid sliding over her shoulder. "Isn't that what memoir is? Walking people straight in?"

Touché.

The truth is, part of me would hand her the keys if it meant she'd know me better. Even if it cost me every ounce of privacy I've fought to keep. But another part, the instinctive father part, recoils at the thought of her digging through my wreckage like it's research material.

I rub the back of my neck. "If you want to write about me… if that helps you with Owen, or the Herald, or whatever—you can. But I don't want to be an assignment to you, Zoe. I don't want to be a test run for your career."

Her lips part, like she hadn't thought of it that way.

I add, softer, "I'd rather just be your dad."

The silence stretches. For once, she doesn't press. She just picks up her fork again, twirling it slowly, eyes darting to the typewriter across the room like it might answer for both of us.

Pretending (Zoe POV)

I poke at my plate, buying myself a second, the lasagna cooling in front of me. He says it so easily, like it isn't terrifying, like it doesn't upend everything.

"Well," I say at last, forcing a small shrug, "maybe it's not a great idea anyway. I mean, at some point people will figure out who you are to me. I guess I'll just tell Owen I'll do something else."

I try to sound casual, like it doesn't matter. But the words taste strange, like they aren't quite mine.

Chapter Sixteen – Fractures

What He Doesn't Know (Jeff POV)

The phone lights up on the counter: Carly.

I almost let it go to voicemail. Almost. But if I don't answer, she'll just keep calling, and the last thing I want is her blowing up Zoe's phone while she's studying.

I swipe. "Carly."

Her voice comes sharp, already charged. "Is she taking the medication?"

I pinch the bridge of my nose. "Yes. She is. She's responsible—"

"Don't you dare tell me she's responsible. You don't know what it's like when she spirals. You don't know what you're doing."

Something tightens in my chest. "Carly, I'm her father. I'm here. I see her. I—"

"You don't know, Jeff. You don't know the nights I sat outside her door, terrified she wouldn't wake up in the morning. You don't know the calls from the school nurse. You don't know the years of walking on eggshells. And you never will."

Her words slice through me. I force myself to keep my voice steady. "She's stronger than you give her credit for."

Carly exhales hard, bitter. "And you're weaker than you admit. Don't spoil her. Don't let her think she can fall apart in your arms and you'll fix it with... with toys. A MacBook won't save her."

Still giving me shit about buying Zoe a computer for school! I resist the urge to tell her off for not taking care of that herself. I get where Carly is coming from, but Zoe is a good kid, a good student. She's far from spoiled. There's something about the way Carly tries to control everything regarding Zoe that rankles with me. No wonder Zoe feels like she doesn't have any space.

My jaw tightens. "She doesn't need saving. She needs believing in."

Silence hums at the other end, sharp as a blade. Then: "You don't know what you're doing," she says one last time, low, and hangs up.

I stare at the dead phone, pulse hammering, anger and guilt knotted until I don't know which one's winning.

The lock clicks.

The door opens.

Zoe steps in, bag slung over her shoulder, but her face—her face is too pale. She doesn't even take her shoes off, just lowers herself to the sofa like gravity's doubled.

"Zo?" I cross the loft in seconds, crouch in front of her. Her chest is rising too fast, shoulders jerking with every breath. I know before she says a word.

She's in it.

I keep my voice low, steady. "I'm here. Look at me. Just breathe with me, okay? In...out."

Her eyes are wild, unfocused, but her hands clutch mine, cold and trembling.

"In...out," I murmur again, exaggerating my own breath so she can follow. "That's it. I've got you."

Her whole body shakes. For a second I think she's going to pass out.

"I've got you," I repeat, firmer this time, anchoring us both.

Fighting (Zoe POV)

The room tilts, air cutting in half. My chest is a locked box and I've lost the key. I can't tell if it's Carly's voice in my head or my own: *You don't know what you're doing. You're too much. You'll ruin this, too.*

Jeff's voice breaks through like a rope thrown down a well. "In...out. With me, Zo."

My lungs spasm, but I try. I hate how broken I must look. I hate that he's seeing me like this, the mess Carly warns him about.

His hands are steady on mine, grounding. His eyes don't flinch. Not pity, not fear. Just there.

The storm rattles, tears blur everything, but slowly—so slowly—the air starts to come back. One breath. Then another. My throat burns. My chest aches. But I'm breathing.

When the sobs finally taper, I collapse forward, forehead against his shoulder, shaking. "I'm sorry," I gasp. I don't even know who I'm apologizing to.

"Don't be sorry." His voice is rough, maybe with his own tears. "Don't ever be sorry for this."

His shirt is damp where my face presses. I almost laugh through the wreck of myself.

"You've got me now," he whispers, simple as that.

And for the first time, I let myself believe it.

Just Beginning (Jeff POV)

Later, after she washes her face and changes into pajamas, we eat the pasta and roasted vegetables I'd grabbed from the deli. I watch her pick at the food, still quiet. She hates me seeing her like that.

Afterward she insists on cleanup. "You cooked. Let me."

"You sure?" I ask, debating whether to make a joke about cooking when it was just reheating.

She nods too quickly. I see it—the way she's trying to prove stability, to be the girl she thinks will keep me around, not the "messy one" she fears will drive me away. She doesn't know how messy I've been, how un-messy she is compared to me.

"Go pick a movie," she says brightly, forced.

I hesitate, debating whether to leave her alone. But she waves me off, determined. So I cross to the shelf of DVDs. I throw myself into it, pretending to debate like it matters. *Annie Hall*? Too complicated. *Some Like It Hot*? Maybe. *The Graduate*? Relevant for the college kid. Amazing soundtrack. *Midnight in Paris*? She loved that last time.

But beneath the browsing, I feel it. Something's still eating at her.

Lying (Zoe POV)

I hear him flipping cases, hear the mutter under his breath. I try to stack plates in neat lines like that will keep my thoughts stacked too. But they sneak in anyway: When I was studying at the cafe down the street, I had a phone call from Julia; she called me about his birthday, May 18. He won't even tell me himself. He shuts me out. He's hot and cold, and I don't know which version will be there tomorrow.

I scrub the counter too hard, breath shaky, fighting to look normal. Stable. Safe.

When I finally join him on the sofa, he glances over. "Can't decide between *Annie Hall* and *Some Like It Hot*."

I shrug like it doesn't matter. "You should pick. It's your birthday soon. The next time we see each other, you'll be what, sixty?"

He laughs, but something flickers in his eyes. Something he hides before I can name it. "Hey, don't put me in the nursing home yet."

I tuck my feet under me, leaning back, forcing myself to smile. If I just act fine, maybe I will be.

Desperation (Jeff POV)

By the time the credits roll, Zoe is curled against the cushions, her breathing slow and even. I don't move. I just sit there, watching her chest rise and fall, afraid that if I shift too much she'll wake. Or worse, that she won't.

When I finally ease myself up, careful not to jostle her, I drape the throw blanket over her shoulders and dim the lamp. She doesn't stir.

I can't sleep. Not tonight.

Back at my desk, I open the laptop and start searching. Panic disorder in adolescents. Panic attacks in college students. Best treatment for panic. Article after article, clinical papers, personal blogs, lists of triggers. I scroll and scroll, chasing answers like a man starved.

Rapid heartbeat, chest tightness, sense of doom. I see her face in every symptom. I type "best panic disorder specialists NYC" into the search bar and bookmark names, numbers, clinics. Half of them I know I'll never call, but I can't stop.

One link leads to another until it's past two a.m., the city outside hushed except for the occasional siren. My eyes burn, but I keep going, jotting notes, compiling resources. Anything that might help me understand what I saw in her tonight—what she's been carrying alone all this time. None of it feels like enough. I want the answer. A cure. A magic fix I can put in my pocket and hand to Zoe the next time she goes pale and breathless. But there isn't one. Every page says the same thing: patience, therapy, management, not elimination.

Eventually, I close the lid and press my hands over my face. I can't fight her panic for her. I know that. But maybe I can fight beside her.

When I finally crawl into bed, dawn feels close. Sleep doesn't come easy. Every time I close my eyes, I see her on the sofa, struggling for air. And I promise myself—next time, I'll be ready.

I lean back, rub my eyes. Patience is useless if she's hurting in front of me and I can't stop it. If I'd been there sooner, maybe I would've known how to help already. I vow, silently, that I'll never be caught unprepared again. Whatever it takes, whoever the best in the world is, I'll find them.

Chapter Seventeen - Withholding

Static & Coping (Zoe POV)

I'm back at the Second Signal Cafe with my new MacBook open. Jeff bought it for me. He said he'd wanted to give it to me for my birthday, but that I seemed to be in need of it immediately. I was embarrassed about it, but honestly, it is a relief not to have to rely on public computers, the school computers, or my suite mates' generosity. I'm trying to outline the last paragraphs of my death penalty paper. The words won't hold still. Julia's voice keeps echoing from yesterday: *His birthday, Zoe. He'll never tell you himself, so I wanted to make sure you knew.*

Why wouldn't he tell me? He doesn't want me to be part of it; that's what I tell myself. One minute I feel like the most important person in his life, and the next I'm invisible. He's cagey about his memoir too, like every word is a locked drawer I'm not allowed to open. Julia means well, but I hate that she's the one who told me. Complicating all of this is the fact that I still haven't gotten him a present. What do you buy for the dad who has everything? I got him a card, but I want to give him something else, something meaningful to express how much…just thinking about my feelings toward Jeff, I'm speechless. It's been such a whirlwind I've hardly had a chance to make sense of it.

My chest tightens. Oh, crap. Not here. Not now. Finals are stacked like bricks on my shoulders, and I can't afford to fall apart. I try breathing the way Dr. Patel showed me. In, out. But Carly's voice still sneaks in, making me feel inadequate. I have been taking the pills, but the panic comes up more than ever and it's only gotten worse since my panic attack in front of Jeff. I hate that he saw me like that and I'm afraid of it happening again. What if he decides I'm too much trouble?

I grip my pen so hard my fingers ache. I am not going to crack open in the middle of the Second Signal Cafe. Not with Augie, the owner, rinsing, wiping, and racking mugs behind the counter. I start doing the five-senses exercise the college physician, Dr. Patel, taught me, looking around at five things to see, four things to touch, three things to hear, two things to smell, and one thing to taste. I touch the table and feel its grooves. I touch my cup, the coffee still in it gone cold, and notice its smoothness. I touch the keys on my MacBook until my pulse finally slows. Three things I can hear, two things I can smell, one thing I can taste. That cold coffee. It does work. My breathing slows. My heartbeat steadies. But I'm hollowed out afterward, still worried it will happen again in front of Jeff.

I'm drinking water when a new email pops up in my college inbox. The sender is Owen Aubrey. Excitedly, almost forgetting my problems, I click on it and read.

Someone Else Making Her Laugh (Jeff POV)

I step into the bursar's office at Roosevelt College — beige carpet, too-bright lights. I slide the folder across the desk: statements, routing numbers, signatures. The 529 is linked now. Tuition covered, books covered, everything covered.

The clerk thanks me briskly. When that's done, I walk out into the quad, students floating by with backpacks and earbuds. Zoe belongs to this world. She shouldn't have to worry about where the money comes from. For the first time, I can give her something solid. A foundation. Not words, not apologies—something that holds.

Still, the guilt tags along: Eighteen years late.

With my finely tuned Zoe-sense, I spot her across the quad, walking on the path from the library to the dorms. There's a guy with her. Owen? For a second, I consider calling out, but something stops me. She and her friend are chatting and smiling. He's making her laugh, which prompts in me an unfamiliar feeling. Jealousy? Why am I jealous? She looks happy. Only it's not me making her feel that way.

Absence (Zoe POV)

"I'm so glad you told me about Griffin," Owen is saying as he holds the door for the dorm open for me. "And I do mean it, MacKenzie. I haven't told anyone."

"I appreciate that, but I am sorry about the interview."

"Don't worry about it," he said. "Trust me when I say we have plenty of articles to write and plenty of people to interview, and, honestly, I'd've had a job of it, speedreading Blackthorn just the article properly."

He seems to regret saying that, I guess because he thinks it's rude not to read one's girlfriend's father's books. It makes me laugh, though. "Oh, you haven't read them?"

He blushes. "I read one of them. *The First Dead Man*? I'm not really interested in the genre."

"That's the first one," I inform him with a laugh. "And to be honest with you, I haven't read them either." I add to myself, *Maybe if I did read his Blackthorn series I could crack the code to understanding him. And I really do want to understand him, even if it does scare the hell out of me.*

"I think we have enough to read," he said. "With finals and everything. So what's left for you? One more final?"

"Yeah, I have to turn in my Writing & Research paper, and then I have the French final, but that's easy."

He nods. We're facing each other now. Other students are walking around us, clamoring up the stairs or waiting for the elevator.

"Are you all packed for your trip?" I ask as a way to deflect from the growing tension, or ease it. It's not like the tension I feel with Jeff. It's more...excitement. Anticipation, I guess. I also don't want Owen to leave, and tomorrow he's going away to London for almost a whole week. I know it's totally logical that he would, it being his home. Owen has a nice family by the sound of it and he likes to see them sometimes. I just really enjoy being around him.

"Yeah, I'm all packed," he replies. "Listen," he begins with a sigh, hitching his thumbs in the pockets of his jeans and nudging his glasses up the bridge of his nose. "I was wondering if...you might, I don't know, keep in touch? We can chat while I'm in London."

"I'd like that," I say, breathing a sigh of relief and smiling. I'm so happy. He wants to keep in touch!

"OK," he says, a huge grin overtaking his face. He pulls out his phone and types out some digits. The ping on my phone alerts me to his text message. It's his number, a long British number. "So now you have my number. Text me yours and then we'll connect through WhatsApp."

As I say goodbye to Owen, I walk up to the third floor in a daze. I think back to our last conversation, when I had to tell him about Jeff because of the fake interview that I'd decided (or Jeff convinced me) not to do, and he was so sweet and understanding about it. He was shocked at first.

"Jeff Griffin? Your dad? Why didn't you tell me before?"

"Well, I myself didn't know until a few weeks ago."

"Oh. I see."

***

By Friday, finals are over. World Civ was a blur of essay prompts; Biology, an avalanche of memorized diagrams; Writing and Research, a slog of words I already know aren't good enough. Maybe I'll pass, maybe I won't.

On the train to Grand Central, exhaustion presses heavier than my bag. By the time I switch to the downtown line, the thought of the Shelley is the only thing carrying me forward. And Owen. Ever since that first email that I read in the Second Signal Cafe, we've been emailing and texting. At first I thought he was only interested in the Jeff Griffin interview. I thought as soon as I told him I couldn't do it, and why, he would drop me like a hot potato. To my amazement, no such thing happened. Owen seems to genuinely like me. I just hope he keeps liking me in London and still likes me when he comes back for the second summer session.

By the time I climb up the subway stairs to the street and head to the Shelley, I'm thinking only about my father and hoping that he'll be more open with me than he was last weekend. Unfortunately, when I push open the door of the loft, it isn't Jeff waiting. It's Nancy, who I recognize from pictures Jeff showed me on his phone.

She's perched on the sofa like a cat who already owns the place. Sharp eyes, sharper smile. "So. You're the daughter."

The way she says it makes me want to shrink. Like she's measuring me, tallying resemblances, deciding what's Jeff and what's Carly.

"He didn't mention you'd be here," I murmur, setting my bag down.

"Jeff's busy," she says smoothly. "But you, let me look at you. You've got his eyes, and something else too. I can't quite put my finger on it."

I force a smile, but unease prickles my skin. Where is he? Why isn't he here?

Anything For You (Jeff POV)

When I finally step through the door, Zoe's sitting rigid on the sofa, and Nancy is all but purring with satisfaction. I feel the air crackle.

Nancy leaves with a kiss on my cheek and a look I don't like. Then Zoe turns on me, her voice trembling but sharp. "What are you hiding from me? You keep saying your past is bad and ugly, but you never tell me anything. You're treating me like Carly does."

Her words land like a slap. I want to comfort her, close the distance, but she backs away. "No. You don't get to just shush me and pretend everything's fine when nothing changes. You're hot, you're cold. You're my dad, you're not going anywhere one minute, and the next it's like...I'm invisible."

I stand frozen. Invisible? To me? Never.

Resolved, I move to the safe built into the wall by my desk. My hands turn the combination that I know by heart. The lock clicks open. Inside: the rough draft, the outline, pages of the memoir I've been circling around. I take it out, feeling her eyes on me, and I hold it like it might burn me.

"Here," I say, offering her the stack of pages, white and yellow ones, held together by a binder clip.

Her eyes widen. "No. It's okay. You don't want me to see it."

"I do want you to see it," I say, baffled. "You're not invisible, Zo. Anything but. This is all for you. I'm writing this for you. Because I want you to know me."

"I wanted you to tell me," she says quickly. "Not for me to drag it out of you or have to read it in a book."

The words cut deep. I tuck the manuscript back into the safe, shut the door. Pretend strength.

"I'm here," I tell her, quiet but steady. "I'll always be here."

Even as I say it, I feel the gap yawning between us, all the truths I still can't give her, because as soon as I do, she'll leave.

Split (Zoe POV)

He says it with such certainty, like the words themselves could anchor me. *I'll always be here.*

Part of me wants to believe it so badly it hurts. The other part whispers that promises are fragile, breakable, like glass.

I nod, because that's what he wants to see, but inside I'm split clean in two—half clinging to his voice, half bracing for the silence that might come next.

***

Later, I'm sitting upstairs, reading his first book in the Blackthorn series. *The First Dead Man*. He actually has a few copies lying around here so I grabbed one. It feels so weird to be reading a book by my dad. Bridget says she read them all, but I never looked at them until now. Even as curious as I've always been about him, I am somewhat afraid of what might be in these books. Sometimes I see people reading them on the subway. Fans see Detective Blackthorn: brooding, relentless, trench coat flapping in the French Quarter rain, or prowling our boroughs. They think that's Jeff Griffin. They think they've caught him.

Me? I get fragments. A promise said too quickly. A silence stretched too long. I live with the man who hides behind the detective, and I'm still guessing at the map of him.

I can't decide which is lonelier: being one of the thousands who know the character, or being the daughter still learning the author.

The covers are always dark and broody, just like him. Jeremy Blackthorn, the protagonist, wears a trench coat and walks around the French Quarter in 1949. I only meant to peek into *The First Dead Man*, but now I'm three chapters in and Blackthorn is walking in alleys I've never seen but somehow feel familiar.

Chapter Eighteen - His Birthday

The Best Gift (Zoe POV)

It's Saturday morning and Jeff is asleep and I'm sitting on the balcony, having hardly slept at all. I just kept reading Dad's book. Detective Blackthorn is eccentric. He's dark and hardly ever smiles. He observes and catalogs things and people, especially women, which is kind of...creepy. Anyway, eventually I fell asleep, the book falling on my face. When I woke up, still tired, I didn't even make coffee because I didn't want to wake him. The sun is coming up. The sky is gorgeous. Orange and yellow and pink. I pad barefoot onto the balcony with my phone, air cool against my skin, and Owen's WhatsApp bubble lighting the screen. It's already mid-afternoon in London.

> Owen: How's the famous Griffin? Nervous about turning the big 4-1?

> Me: He hasn't said a word. Pretends it's just another day.

> Owen: You'll break through. That's what daughters do.

I bite my lip, tapping back a smiley I don't quite feel.

Part of me is now regretting that I told Owen about Jeff being my father. The number of people who know is growing too fast for my liking. At the same time, it's great to have someone like Owen, who is so easy to talk to. He's so...easy. I mean, his life is easy. He has a mom and a dad who are actually married. They have what they call a "flat" in Notting Hill. I want to go to England someday and see where Jane Austen wrote her incredible novels. I've read them all, even the Juvenilia and her Letters. I found a few of her titles among Jeff's books one day and asked him about it. He said he admires the way Austen really understands human nature.

The door slides open behind me. Jeff steps out, hair still sleep-tousled, carrying two mugs of coffee like he read my mind. His eyes crease. "Happy morning."

"Happy birthday," I say quickly, before nerves can steal it from me.

He pauses, surprised, then chuckles. "You remembered."

"Of course I remembered. I, um—can I give you your present now? Not at the party. Just us."

He nods, puzzled. I lead him inside to the piano. Heart hammering, I lift the lid and set out the sheet I'd found tucked deep in his father's music book: a half-written jazz melody, scrawled over with corrections. His dad's handwriting.

I play it, the way I've practiced in secret at school. The notes are hesitant at first, then loosen, flowing with his father's scribbled revisions, carrying something alive from one Griffin to the next.

When I finish, silence holds. Jeff's eyes shine. He swallows, voice rough. "Come here."

I go, and he wraps me in his arms. His chest shakes.

"I'm sorry," I whisper. "I thought you'd like it."

"Like it?" His laugh breaks, quiet and broken. "It's the best gift I've ever been given."

He doesn't let go, and neither do I.

The Worst Fear (Jeff POV)

I want to tell her everything. Holding her, I want to spill the whole ugly truth, the things I've carried like stones in my chest for years. But I don't. If I tell her, I could lose this. Lose her. And that terrifies me more than silence.

So I just hold on.

I want to tell her everything. Holding her, I think: this is where the book should begin—her hands on my father's melody. I am forty-one and I still believe silence can protect the people I love. It never has. It only convinces them I am not there.

The Beach (Zoe POV)

Later, the motorcycle roars beneath us, carrying us out of Manhattan. The wind whips my braid, and my arms wrap tight around his waist. For a moment I feel free—until I feel him retreat, quiet again after the music.

By the time we reach the house the Logans—his sister Nancy, her husband Cole Logan and their sons, his nephews, my cousins—are staying at in the Hamptons, guests are already spilling onto the beach. Theo and Julia wave from the porch, her belly round now, seven months, hands resting protectively on it.

"Zoe!" Julia greets me like an old friend, pulling me aside with that calm therapist energy that sees too much. She chats, gentle, until I feel her eyes flicker, reading the edge in me I try to hide. "You know," she says softly, "anxiety isn't weakness. It's just your body asking for help. Don't shame it. Learn its language."

I nod, throat tight.

Down on the sand, Theo signs at me, grinning, [I'm throwing it to you.]

A nerf football soars through the air, wobbling. I catch it clumsily but the boys—Cole Jr. and Wyatt—cheer like I scored a touchdown.

Jeff is watching. I see his shoulders ease when I laugh.

Cousins (Jeff POV)

She's holding her own. Not panicking, not retreating. Playing with my nephews, standing in the sun like she belongs here. I don't hear their words, but I see enough: Wyatt's gentleness, Cole Jr. peppering her with questions. And Zoe answering—actually answering—without running.

My chest aches with pride.

Excluded (Zoe POV)

Evening comes. We gather on the terrace. Julia brings out a cake from the city bakery—shaped like a typewriter, candles 4 and 1 glowing on top. Everyone claps as Jeff leans over them.

He closes his eyes. Makes a wish. Blows them out.

I clap with the rest, but something knots in me.

Presents follow: a baseball cap with a Ducati logo on it from Theo, a bottle of wine from Cole, expensive watch from Nancy, baby clothes from Julia "so you'll have to babysit." Laughter all around.

Then Jeff stands, clears his throat, glass in hand. "Thank you," he says. "For making an old man feel young. I'm grateful—for family, for friendship, for second chances."

He names them one by one. Theo, Julia, Cole, Nancy, the boys. But not me. His eyes glance my way, then away. My face burns.

Singled Out in Silence (Jeff POV)

I don't name her. I don't want to put her on the spot, don't want to drag her into questions. But the omission hangs heavy. I feel it even as the room laughs.

From the Fragments of the Unpublished Memoir of Jeff Griffin:

Silence is not absence. It is a posture. At our kitchen table in Baton Rouge, silence meant listening. In New York, it became hiding. I learned to keep whole months unspoken because if I didn't say it, it couldn't be used against anyone I loved. That's the lie. Secrets weigh the same whether you carry them or confess them. They just bruise you in different places.

Despair (Zoe POV)

The ride back on the bike is quiet. At the loft, I retreat to my little room, shower running hot until steam fills the glass. Only then do I cry, sobbing into the spray, muffling it in the sound of water. Finally letting it out.

Later I hear him pacing below. He doesn't ask. I don't tell. We both go to bed with heavy hearts. I'm not even in the mood to read more of *The First Dead Man*.

Chapter Nineteen — Losing the Signal

Seeking Advice (Zoe POV)

I leave the note on the fridge—Went for coffee. Don't worry—and slip out before sunrise. The streets are cool and gray and empty, the kind of quiet New York only gives you if you wake up indecently early or never sleep.

Owen's WhatsApp bubble lights as I hit the corner.

> Owen: Morning, MacKenzie.
>
> Me: Afternoon, London.
>
> Owen: How's post-party Jeff?
>
> Me: Complicated.
>
> Owen: You two will find the gear. You will.

I circle the block twice just to keep talking. He listens without prying, like he's learned the trick of making space on a phone line.

By the third loop, the coffee smell from the Second Signal Cafe hooks me inside.

Augie clocks me the second the bell tinks. "MacKenzie. You look like a storm that almost happened."

"Almost," I say.

He slides me a mug. "Which truck hit you this time?"

"The birthday." The words come easier here. Augie knows what I'm referring to because I discussed birthday ideas with him. It was Augie who gave me the idea of doing something sentimental instead of buying something. Now I tell him about Jeff's birthday speech. "He thanked everyone. Not me." I shake my head. "I know he didn't mean to. But it stuck."

Augie leans on the counter, unbothered by long silences. "Some folks love like they're carrying a box of glass. Too careful, end up dropping it anyway."

"I played him something," I blurt. "From his dad's old book. He cried."

"Then the gift landed," Augie says. "Don't let a clumsy toast rewrite that truth."

I nod, let the warmth from the mug work its way into my fingers. "Okay."

"Eat," he orders, sliding over a croissant. "You can't fight shadows on caffeine alone."

I thank him, pocket his words, and head back.

She comes in with an iced coffee sweating down her hand and a paper bag she treats like treasure. Keys clatter on the counter.

"I was at Second Signal," she says, like it's the most ordinary thing in the world. Maybe it is.

She opens the bag and holds out a croissant. "Want some?"

"Thanks." I take it, careful not to brush her fingers. But what I'm really noticing is how she always goes there. Early. Alone. Like a ritual she didn't ask my blessing for and doesn't need.

I think of her on the balcony last week, phone lit against dawn. London mornings overlap with New York dawn. Owen. Augie at the Second Signal Cafe.

I want to ask, *Why there? Why always there?* But questions can turn into fences. I don't want to be a fence.

So I take another bite and pretend I don't care.

I do. God, I do.

From the Fragments of the Unpublished Memoir of Jeff Griffin:

Fatherhood at forty-one is learning to love without proof. It is restraint as devotion. It is wanting to ask and choosing to wait. It is standing in a room with an open door and praying she walks through of her own will. It is pretending not to care about a croissant because questions feel like fences and you promised yourself you would not be a fence.

Second Opinion (Zoe POV)

A week later, I'm starting the first summer session at Roosevelt College. The dorms are half-empty; the classrooms are not. Owen is still in London. He'll be back to do the second summer session. On the first day of classes, I climb the short flight to Dr. Allison Lawson's office in The Castle. Her door is propped with a copy of Gibbon.

She pours tea and studies me with that unwavering look that makes lying feel like yelling in a church.

"How's Jeff?" she asks, like she's taking a pulse. (She and Owen are the two people I've told about my new father.)

"Complicated," I say.

"Complicated how?"

"He opens up and then he disappears. It's like a door in him swings shut." I swallow. "At his birthday he… forgot me. Or he didn't say my name. Which maybe isn't the same as forgetting, but it felt like it."

Lawson lets the words hang. Then: "Maybe it's not where you stand with him. Maybe it's where he stands with himself."

I frown. "I don't know what that means."

"Boundaries aren't just about keeping people out," she says. "They're markers so you don't lose yourself. If his silence hurts, you can name that. You can say: 'I can't sit in the dark and wait. I need light, or I'm going to walk away.' That's drawing your line. Not to control him. To protect you."

"What if he leaves?" I whisper.

"What if he doesn't?" she counters gently. "What if he meets you on level ground?"

I nod like I understand. I don't, not fully. But her words drop into me like stones in water—sinking, making rings I'll feel later.

I leave with the taste of Earl Grey and a sentence I don't know how to finish: Draw your own line.

Chapter Twenty — Signals and Lines

Drawing a Line (Zoe POV)

After class on Friday, I don't get on the train to Grand Central. Instead, I walk into town. In the Bronxville bookstore and cafe, where I first saw and spoke to Jeff, I choose a corner table where the light hits the dust in soft columns. The MacBook glows. The cursor blinks. Neutral ground, except it isn't. Everything started here.

I think of Dr. Lawson's line: Draw your own line. It's a boundary, not for him or to control him, but to protect me. I think of Augie's advice: don't let clumsiness masquerade as rejection. I think of Jeff's eyes when I played him the music from his father. My grandfather, Paul Griffin, a lawyer who collected stamps, played piano, and fixed old cars.

I'm having trouble drafting an email I want to send to Jeff. Where do I even begin? And then it hits me: I begin at the beginning, same as coming here to this bookstore and coffee shop, the place I first interacted with him. The place I dropped the names of his past, got his attention. I log into my Roosevelt email and start a new message:

I stop. The café noise rushes back in. I sip a latte gone cold.

The line Dr. Lawson gave me presses against my ribs. I don't know yet how to write it—where my line is, how to ask for light without blowing out the candles—but I can feel the outline of it, faint as a watermark.

I add one more paragraph.

> *I don't need you to fix me. I just need you to let me see you. If you can't, tell me you can't. I'll try to be brave about that. But please don't keep me in the dark and call it protection. I can't breathe there.*

I read it three times, then I don't send it. I save it as a draft and tuck the thought away like a match I'm not ready to strike.

I stare at my phone. My pulse hammers. I know what I have to do, but making myself do it? That's the impossible part. I need space. I need air. I need to know what's happening between us. It's like we're stuck in the static again.

Resolved—or pretending I am—I pick up the phone and call Jeff.

He answers on the first ring. "Hey, kid. You almost here?"

His voice is warm, expectant. Hopeful.

My throat tightens. The word catches like a burr. Finally, I force it out. "No."

A pause. "No? What do you mean?" I hear the fear threading through his voice.

"I'm not coming this weekend."

Silence. I squeeze my eyes shut. Say something, anything, make it less cruel.

"Why not?" he asks, softer now.

"I just… need to figure some things out."

Another silence. Long, stretching, unbearable. I know I'm hurting him and I hate myself for it. I picture him alone in the loft, jaw set, holding himself together by a thread.

"OK," he finally says. The word lands heavy. "Whatever you need."

But underneath it, I hear the crack—supportive and broken at the same time.

"Thanks."

"Zoe?"

"Yeah?"

The line hums with his silence. My chest aches with the weight of everything unsaid. Finally, he speaks, quiet and final:

"Take care."

It's like a bullet tearing through me. Did I just lose him?

"You too." My voice fractures on the last word, and then I hang up.

Chapter Twenty-One — Lost

The line goes dead.

I just sit there, phone still to my ear, as if maybe she'll call back. Maybe it's a mistake. Maybe the silence will shatter with her voice again. But it doesn't.

The loft feels too big, like the walls are leaning back to make more room for the echo of her absence. My hand drops the phone onto the counter, a dull clatter, and I reach automatically for the bottle already sitting there. I don't even bother with a glass this time.

I lost her.

The thought hits me with the force of a hammer, over and over, until it's the only thing I can hear. I had her here, safe, and I fucked it up. Pushed too hard, not enough, the wrong things, all of it. Just like Carly said. Just like everyone who ever—

She says she isn't coming.

It's one sentence over a thin phone line and it knocks the air out of my chest. I'm standing by the kitchen island, one hand on the marble like the room just tilted.

"Why not?" I hear myself ask, too quickly, too loud.

"I just... need to figure some things out."

Silence. I can hear the building hum, the elevator cables somewhere in the shaft, the city flicking its lights on and off like distant signals. I swallow.

"Okay," I say finally. "Whatever you need."

"Thanks."

"Zoe?"

"Yeah?"

Another silence, longer. If I say 'I love you', it might sound like a plea. If I say 'take your time', it might sound like a door closing. I promised myself I would never be a fence! I would never block her. I would never take away her freedom, her safety, her choices. I land on the smallest thing that still feels true.

"Take care."

"It's like a bullet," she says—only she doesn't. I hear it anyway. The line clicks. The room is too quiet.

I put the phone down. I take it back up. I put it down again. The loft stretches out around me: brick, beams, the firehouse pole lit in a stripe of evening. A city for two that suddenly feels like a museum after hours.

I pour a drink I don't need. Then another I definitely don't.

Dylan scratches the air from the old speakers — "Not Dark Yet" because apparently I want to make a meal of the mood. I try pacing; I fail at it. I try writing; the cursor blinks like it's mocking me. The typewriter watches from the desk: stubborn, loyal iron. I can't touch it.

The last thing I wrote, before I lost everything:

The taxi door was open. I looked up and saw her across the street, and the street fell away. There are moments when the past writes its name on the present so clearly you don't need ink. I have built a life on deciding when to cross and when to stay on the curb. That day I learned what it is to be pulled. There are choices that are not choices at all.

I drink until the edges blur. The memoir pages sit scattered across the desk, mocking me. What's the point of dragging my past into the light if I've already failed at the only thing that mattered in the present?

The piano across the loft is silent. The bed upstairs, her bed is empty. She should be here, filling this space with the sound of her laugh, her music, her presence. Instead there's just me, the typewriter quiet, the keys untouched, and the bottle running low.

> TEXT MESSAGE FROM THEO: Two writers walk into a bar

I don't reply. Five minutes later....

ANOTHER TEXT FROM THEO: One anemic, his name is E, he says, I want to get better.

Two minutes later....

ANOTHER TEXT FROM THEO: The other writer says, Well, you need some Iron, E.

I don't know how much time passes before Julia is calling. I let it go to voicemail.

Her voicemail comes in. I read the transcript: "Um, hi. Jeff, give us a call, ok?"

By the time the knock comes, I'm slouched against the desk, papers on the floor, the room spinning just enough to make standing a challenge. It's not Zoe. Of course it's not Zoe.

It's Julia's voice, muffled through the door. "Jeff? Open up."

I close my eyes. Shame burns hot under the alcohol fog. They know. Somehow they always know.

I stagger to the door and unlatch it, and there they are— Theo with his furrowed brow, Julia with her hand resting instinctively against her stomach. The sight of them undoes me in a way the whiskey couldn't.

Theo is there when I swing it wide—bald spot catching the hall light, eyes taking me in, a quick scan that lands on the bottle by the sink, then back to my face. Julia slips past me with a breath and goes straight to the counter like she owns the place, scooping up the half-empty bottle from the counter and pouring all of it in the sink.

I sign before I speak, clumsy with the whiskey.

[Where's the fire?], I try for a smile.

Theo doesn't buy it. He taps two fingers to his chest:
[You]. Then a flat palm, steady: [We're not going
anywhere.]

I want to argue, to tell them I'm finished, that I've lost
everything worth holding on to. But the words won't
come. All I can manage is a broken laugh, a shake of my
head.

And then, with the weight of their presence filling the
hollow loft, I finally let myself unravel.

***

Theo gets me to the sofa like I'm a drunk who just
stumbled out of some dive bar at two a.m. Julia follows
behind.

"I don't need a babysitter," I mutter, though my voice
cracks halfway through.

[You don't need to be alone either], Theo signs back. He's
not angry, but he's firm, immovable. He takes the
armchair opposite me, planting himself like a wall.

"I am alone. Zoe's not coming. I lost her. I screwed up. I
knew I would and now it's happening. I knew I couldn't
be a dad, that I'd fail just like I've failed at everything else
that means any goddamn thing."

Julia sits closer, perched on the edge of the sofa, her hand light on my arm. "Jeff, listen. She's not gone. This isn't the end. She loves you."

I drag both hands over my face. My head throbs, a dull drumbeat. "You didn't hear her. The way she said it. She doesn't want me."

"You're her father," Julia says, calm as ever. "She wants you more than she knows how to admit."

"Bullshit," I snap, sharper than I intend, but I can't pull it back. "You didn't hear her voice. You didn't feel—" I choke off, chest tightening. "I lost her. Just like I lose everything."

Theo leans forward, elbows on his knees. He signs: [Jeff. Stop. You didn't lose her. She's breathing. She's alive. And she's still here, even if she needs space].

Space. The word makes me want to punch something. Space is distance. Distance is loss.

I laugh, broken, ugly. "You don't get it. She's my—" The word sticks in my throat, too small for what I feel. "She's my kid. My only chance to do something right. And I've already ruined it."

Julia's eyes soften, but she doesn't let me turn away. "Why don't you just tell us what happened."

The silence after that hangs heavy. Theo stands, crosses to the desk, starts quietly stacking the scattered pages of my memoir into a neat pile. His movements are methodical, grounding, as if order on the desk can bring order to me.

Julia doesn't move. She stays right there beside me, her hand steady against my sleeve, her presence both unbearable and necessary.

I want them gone. I want them to stay. I want Zoe here, and the fact that she isn't is a hole in my chest that nothing can fill.

Since I don't have the whiskey bottle anymore, to distract myself from the pain, I recount the conversation, my daughter's words: "Not coming. Need to figure some things out. She doesn't need me anymore."

"Jeff, no," Julia says firmly. "That's not true. She's never going to stop needing you. That's not how parenthood works."

I shake my head, eyes burning. "I don't believe that. She has a boyfriend now. He makes her laugh. I don't make her laugh anymore. She can't get out of here fast enough. The coffee shop. Augie."

"Augie? Is he the boyfriend?"

"No, he owns the coffee shop. The Second Signal Cafe. What kind of name is that? It's the name of the coffee shop my daughter runs to get away from me."

"OK, that's it. I'm calling her."

Theo rushes over and they start arguing, Theo reading her lips and then signing back. He thinks calling Zoe is a bad idea. Julia thinks we need to hear the whole story.

I want Julia to contact Zoe, but I don't believe it will do any good if she does. And so I sit there between them, unraveling, every muscle aching with the need for my daughter's presence, while Theo and Julia refuse to let me vanish into the dark.

***

We're sitting on my floor. Julia sits on the rug and tucks her legs under her. Theo leans back against the sofa, ankles crossed, translating my chopped-up sentences into something that sounds less like a confession and more like air.

"I'm losing her," I say, and the words taste like blood.

"No," Julia says, soft but sure. "You scared her. Those are different things."

I want to argue, but my body gives out first. Sometime after midnight I knock out in the chair by the window with the skyline like a bruise. When I surface in the dark, the clock on the oven says 2:17. The loft is quiet. Theo and Julia are upstairs in the nook—two silhouettes where Zoe should be, one small curve of her belly under the throw. For a second I think I dreamed everything.

My phone glows on the counter.

>   *Subject: (no subject)*

>   *From: Zoe*

I read it once, hunched over the counter, the blue light making my hands look like they belong to someone else. I read it again standing up straight, heart in my throat. I read it a third time with my eyes closed.

Dad,

I know you think I'm leaving, that I'm walking away. I don't know how to prove to you that I'm not. I don't even know if you'll believe me. You're really stubborn, you know that? I guess I am too. I don't know what you're so afraid of me finding out. I guess you think I'm really fragile and maybe I am. Maybe if I learn something really bad about you it'll break me. I doubt it, but how can I know if you won't tell me? So let's just assume that whatever it is you don't want me to know is bad enough that if I knew I'd bolt. Here's the thing. As bad as that could be, I doubt it would be worse than this place you're leaving me in right now—this place where I'm in a cage that you made for me, to "protect" me, but since you won't tell me anything I just have to sit here in this cage, alone and untouched. I'm the girl you don't mention because you don't want to break me. It's not like Carly, but, Jeff, actually it is. Your reasons are different, but the effect is the same. Carly's answer was to keep me in a box where she could control me and make sure I was doing what I needed to do in order to not fall apart. Your answer is to keep this huge part of yourself closed off from me even while you dangle it in my face and you tell me you're doing it for me. I can't breathe in here, Jeff. This is my line. I don't want to lose you, but I won't stay in the dark.

Because, honestly, Jeff, I feel like I've lost you anyway. I love you and that's why I have to tell you these things. Otherwise I could just stay in the dark and let you buy me things and live like a shadow in your loft. I can't do that. I need my father, whole. The whole package. In fragments, that's fine, but not put in my hands when you don't want to give them because you're afraid I'll walk out the door.

Love,

Z

I don't answer. Not yet. If I write now I'll either say everything or nothing, and both are wrong. I leave a note for Theo and Julia on the kitchen island—'Went for a run. Back soon'—and lace my shoes.

Outside, the city is a river of concrete and sodium, and the air tastes damp, almost clean. I jog west until the Hudson opens and the wind moves through me like a hand pressing my chest and letting go.

I put on a song she loves. Coldplay. "Fix You." I hate how on the nose it is. I let it play anyway. At the first guitar swell, something breaks open in me and all that's left is breath, feet, breath, feet, breath. I run until the eastern sky goes from ink to steel to the faintest hint of gold on the lip of the water.

When I cut back toward SoHo, the shutters on the Second Signal Cafe are still down. I keep walking, making slow laps around the block, a man with nowhere to be and everywhere to go. At six, Augie cranks the gate up. He looks at me like he's been expecting me.

"You look like you need something strong," he says. "Coffee. The other stuff, you should leave to the amateurs."

I almost laugh. "Black," I say.

He pours. He doesn't ask. He just waits, the way old trees wait out storms.

"You get many sunrises?" I ask, because I don't know how to talk about anything else.

"I get all of them," he says. "It's the tax on owning a coffee shop."

He doesn't say her name. He doesn't say mine. He glances toward the corner table where a certain girl likes the light.

"She was in a few times," he says, eyes staying on the steam rising from my mug. "Kid loves her pop. Doesn't know how to reach him. You hear things when you refill cups."

I breathe through my nose. It hurts less that way.

"I shut my kids out," Augie adds, like a man dropping a coin in a confession box. "Didn't want them to see me break. Turned out it's what broke us."

The mug warms my hands in a way that feels medicinal. "Thanks," I say.

"For the coffee?"

"For the sermon."

He smirks. "You're in the right neighborhood for sermons."

When I get back, Theo is at the island with the note held up like a citation. [Where's your parole officer?], he signs, deadpan.

"Getting scolded by a barista," I say.

Julia pads out from the bathroom, hair wet, eyes kind. "Did you sleep?"

"No. Zoe sent me an email."

"Did you read it?"

"Yes."

"Good," she says. "Then answer her."

Theo nods. He signs it slower, making each word an anchor: [Answer. Her.]

I carry the phone to the balcony. The city is fully awake now, small figures on the street moving like sheet music. I put my back to the brick and type like I'm afraid the words will run if I look directly at them.

> *Subject: The door*

> *Zo,*

I heard you. I've been holding the door like a guard instead of opening it like a father. That's on me.

I'm scared. Not of you, not even of the ugly parts— of losing you again if I get this wrong. But I'm more scared of letting you live in the dark. If you'll let me, I'll do this slowly and honestly. Not fragments thrown into your hands. Pieces, together.

May I start by telling you a story?

— Dad

I hover over send like I'm standing on a ledge. Then I jump.

The phone is suddenly heavy and useless. I stay out there until the brick warms at my back and the breath in my chest finally decides to keep showing up.

The reply arrives with the sun shining bright on the balcony, a little ping that feels like a bell at vespers.

Subject: Re: The door

Dad,

I don't know how to do this either.

Remember when you asked if you could just be my dad?

Maybe start there.

— Z

I don't cry. Not then. I take the phone inside like it's something alive and set it on the counter between the three of us. Theo reads it. Julia reads it. No one says anything for a long time.

I make waffles for three. I burn the first batch. It feels like a sacrament anyway.

Chapter Twenty-Two — Fragments (Zoe POV)

Between classes and subway rides and the long quiet nights where we're both trying not to say too much too fast, we write.

Email is safer than breathing in the same room. It gives us an inch between the heart and the mouth. We use it.

The Emails

ZOE → DAD

> Subject: Dr. Lawson's definition of summer fun
>
> Dad,
>
> One book a week. She wasn't kidding. This week: *The French Revolution: A Very Short Introduction.* "Very short" = 500 pages of guillotines and bread riots. I'm halfway through and now I'm craving carbs. Do you think the revolution could've been avoided if Paris had more bagel shops?
>
> — Z

Subject: Bread and circuses

Zo,

Don't knock bread riots. Without them, no *Les Mis*. Without *Les Mis*, no Gavroche. Without Gavroche, thirteen-year-old me has nothing to cry over while pretending to read *The Great Gatsby*.

And yes, bagels might have saved France. Cinnamon-raisin diplomacy? I'll write to my congressman.

Love,

Dad

Subject: Franny & Zooey (spelled wrong, obviously)

Started Salinger. I don't know how I feel about a book that uses my name but spells it wrong. I feel robbed. On the other hand, Franny melting down in a restaurant bathroom felt… uncomfortably relatable. If you see me carrying a "Jesus Prayer," intervene.

Z

Subject: How to major in everything

Franny's prayer is a smoke alarm—annoying until you need it.

Good thing about English and History: both teach you to argue about bread riots and bathroom breakdowns. If you can connect Robespierre to Salinger in a single sentence, you're ready for grad school. Or politics. Or Thanksgiving.

Also—don't panic about majors. They're just names for excuses to keep reading.

Dad

Subject: Not panicking. Totally not.

Totally not panicking about majors. Not at all. Nope. I'm fine.

...Okay maybe a little.

Z

Between those jokes, he starts slipping small stories into the cracks, each one no bigger than a postcard.

Subject: Story #1 — The Jelly Rescue

When I was six Nancy put a jar of grape jelly on the top shelf "so Jeff won't eat it straight from the spoon." I climbed onto the counter and the whole shelf came down like a guillotine built by Sears. Mom walked in to find a boy covered in jelly, an apostle of purple panic. She didn't yell. She handed me a spoon and said, "If you're going to make a mess, make it at the table."

I've been trying to live at the table ever since.

Dad

Subject: Verdict on the Jelly Rescue

That's adorable and also explains a lot about your waffle policies.

Also: I bought grape jelly. It felt like homework.

Z

Subject: Story #2 — The Typewriter

Your grandfather's music book—the one you found—sat in a box for years. I kept telling myself I'd learn his songs before I was old. Turns out you can get old while you're making those promises. That's why I bought the typewriter. It's a dumb shrine, maybe. Or a way of telling myself to stop waiting to deserve the work.

Dad

Subject: Not dumb

Shrines aren't dumb if they make you brave. Also, I'm practicing your dad's melody when you're not around, so when I play it for you again it doesn't sound like a cat in distress.

Z

He keeps going. A paragraph here, a paragraph there. Nothing gory. Nothing that turns the world upside down. Just enough truth to breathe by.

Subject: Story #3 — Third Grade

Theo and I met because I was the only kid who tried to sign "good morning" and accidentally signed "potato." He laughed so hard he fell off his chair. He was the first person who didn't correct me before including me. That matters.

Dad

Subject: Potatoes & people

I like that you're the kind of person who tries (and fails) instead of the kind who waits until he's perfect.

Z

Subject: Story #4 — First Rejection

I pinned my first rejection letter above the desk with a thumbtack like it was a diploma. I thought it would hurt less if I could see it. It still hurt. But every time I saw it I thought, "I'm the sort of person who gets rejected for writing." Which was almost like "I'm the sort of person who writes."

Dad

Subject: Exhibit A

This is why I'm not terrified of my paper anymore. (Only mildly terrified.)

P.S. The French Revolution definitely needed bagels.

Z

Some days there are only two lines.

Subject: Re: Today

Ate lunch at the counter. Thought about you.

Dad

Subject: Today

Read in the park between classes. Thought about you.

Z

And sometimes, when I don't expect it, he opens the door a little wider.

Subject: Story #5 — Your Name

I didn't know your name. For eighteen years I didn't know your name. I walked through bookstores and looked for it on dedications and

acknowledgments and I wrote your absence into
men who were angry for reasons they couldn't
name. I thought if I kept writing that ache,
someday the ache would answer back. You did.

Dad

I stare at that one for a long time before I answer. I think
this one is my favorite. When he talks about writing my
absence into men, I wonder if he's talking about the
silence, about Blackthorn moving through the French
Quarter in The First Dead Man.

It makes me want to go back to the book and read closer.
To see if I can find myself in the shadows he left behind.

But I'm not sure if I'll ever tell him I'm reading it. What if
he doesn't want me to? What if he does?

ZOE → DAD

Subject: Re: Your Name

You named me anyway. Zo. I don't really know
what to say, except...thank you.

I like this one. A lot.

Z

We try not to rush it. We fail at that sometimes. But
mostly, we keep to small things—bread, books, light.

He sends a picture of the stamp album opened on the
kitchen table, a page of countries that don't exist
anymore; I send a picture of my marginalia crawling up
the spine of Franny and Zooey. He sends a sentence he

likes and dares me to finish it. I send him a line from my paper that doesn't embarrass me.

On Thursday night, after I close my laptop and stare at the ceiling in the dim light of the dorm, my phone pings again.

DAD → ZOE

> Subject: Friday?
>
> Just waffles. No fragments. No speeches. Just waffles.
>
> Dad

I don't make him wait.

ZOE → DAD

> Subject: Re: Friday
>
> Yes.
>
> Z

Between send and sunrise, I sleep like a person who has decided—if only for a weekend—that the door is open and the light is on.

Chapter Twenty-Three – Planning the Nineteenth

Safety (Jeff POV)

Bridget's voice on the phone is calm, almost conspiratorial. "August third, Jeff," as if I needed reminding. "We have to plan Zoe's birthday party. A surprise. 19 years old. Carly and I thought we'd all do something up there."

Up there. New York. My turf, but already halfway theirs.

I glance around the loft, picturing it packed with them—Bridget's clipped precision, Carly's watchful disapproval, Zoe's bright presence at the center, maybe a few of her friends. "The loft works," I say. "My building has a rooftop garden. Excellent view. Could be nice. Great for a summer party. I'll make sure it's set up."

Bridget exhales, relieved. "Good. We'll coordinate details. Just... keep Zoe in the dark."

Keep Zoe in the dark. That will be the hard part. The rest is just logistics.

When the call ends, I leave my laptop open to the blank search bar where I've typed 'a safe car for a college student.' Glossy images of shiny new cars overtake the screen—Audis, Toyotas, Volvos, Subarus. Five-star crash ratings. Side-impact tests. Blind spot monitoring. Things I never thought twice about in my own twenties but can't stop obsessing over now. I can see Zoe behind the wheel, hair caught in the wind, finally free in a way she's never been allowed to be.

Then Carly's voice from our last conversation cuts through the fantasy—cold as a courthouse hallway: "I don't want to spoil her, Jeff. A car is too extravagant."

"She deserves—" I'd started.

"She deserves stability, not indulgence. She isn't a prize to be bought."

I swallowed the reply. The line went dead, but the weight stuck.

I flip between tabs, Consumer Reports, safety blogs, dealership sites. The MacBook screen glows against the dim loft. Every car looks like a lifeline, a way to shield her from a world I can't control.

Carly's voice echoes in my head—*She doesn't need a car in New York, Jeff. It's too extravagant. It'll go to her head.* Bridget's is softer but just as maddening: *Safe doesn't mean spoiled. She needs boundaries.*

In a way, Bridget's calm annoys me more than Carly's bitchiness. At least Carly has a right to interfere. I put up with all of it because creating a war with Zoe's lifelong maternal figures won't make anything better, but I won't let them deter me from what feels right.

They don't get it. It isn't about indulgence. It's about independence. About not having to ride the late train alone, not waiting on sidewalks in the dark. It's about Zoe getting into something with reinforced steel and airbags and making it home safe.

I picture her behind the wheel, windows down, music up. Her music, not mine. Freedom without strings. A machine that says: you don't have to wait on anyone. Not Carly. Not Bridget. Not even me.

Carly, Bridget, and I are in regular touch nowadays. Zoe and I are back in the routine we started in May. It's now the middle of July, the second summer session in full swing, and Owen Aubrey back in her life. Her birthday looms ahead. Exciting. Terrifying. Her first with me in her life, her 19th overall. I wonder what it will be like to say 'my 19-year-old daughter' when I've hardly gotten used to saying 'my 18-year-old daughter.'

I scroll through the search results on the Volvo site, hovering over the order button. Volvo XC40. Electric. Top safety ratings. The kind of car an environmentally conscious father buys when he wants his daughter safe.

I rub my eyes, scroll back to the top. My hand hovers over a button—Schedule test drive. Not yet. I want to pick the right one. The best one. The one that buys me peace of mind, even if it earns me Carly's fury.

The decision's already made. I'm giving her a car. Carly can fight me later.

I close the laptop and lean back, staring at the dark ceiling beams. I've given her a desk, a bed, a MacBook. All good. All useful. But this? This would be the thing that tells her I trust her out there in the world.

Carly can rage. Bridget can scold. To hell with their permission. End of story. Zoe deserves more than trains and borrowed rides.

She deserves the wheel.

Strength (Zoe POV)

By the middle of July, the air on campus feels different. The days are slower somehow, everything stretched thin by the heat, even the trees sagging under the glare of the sun. Owen is back; that's something. Although, as I take my seat beside him in my Russian Revolution class, I'm already missing Dr. Lawson. Instead, her TA, Regina Spencer, is teaching the class. She's a sharp-eyed, perfectionist grad student with an accent from South America. She's knowledgeable, but remote, passionate about the subject but disinterested in the audience. She talks quickly and I try to keep up, scribbling random observations about the speaker in my notebook:

> *Brittle, never laughs, appropriate—after all,*
> *Revolutions aren't funny.*

I can't help missing the very air in Dr. Lawson's classroom, thick with the smell of chalk and summer dust, while she paced the front of the room, lecturing about the French Revolution like she was there personally, whispering to Robespierre. "Revolutions are born not from hunger alone," she declared, "but from the imagination of people who believe things could be otherwise." Regina Spencer doesn't use a chalkboard. She doesn't make the events feel like they're happening in the room. I don't begrudge Dr. Lawson taking a break. She deserves it. I just miss her.

I'm using the same notebook here that I used in the French Revolution class. Sometimes I notice my old margin scribbles, phrases caught from Dr. Lawson like precious nuggets of wisdom. In my notes about why revolutions happen, I took note of the words:

> *imagination—believing things could be otherwise.*

Later, in French Lit, I curl into the back row with a thin paperback of Camus. The absurd weighs on me, but also frees me. Last night, I'd had an email from Dad, after I'd sent one in which I remarked that I find Camus depressing. He disagreed: "He's not depressing, he's liberating. The pointlessness is the point. It means you get to decide what matters."

At lunch, I tell Owen, "You wouldn't believe it. Camus makes despair sound like an aesthetic. I half want to smoke a cigarette in a trench coat just to do him justice."

Owen leans back, amused. "Finally. Someone gets it. French literature is just therapy disguised as philosophy."

I grin, warmed by his presence. I'm amazed how acutely I felt his absence, how attached I've become to the way he looks at me.

We spill out into the quad. His questions start flying, as always. "So tell me about last session's lit—did you like Salinger? Or were you just pretending so you didn't fail?"

"First of all, Franny and Zooey isn't about me, no matter how many times you wink when you say 'Zooey.'"

"That's a shame," he grins. "Because you'd have made Salinger a fortune."

I have no idea what he means by that, but his accent makes everything sound true and amazing. I smile up at him. "I'm glad you're back, and that we have Russian Revolution together."

"Me too," he says, and I know he's revving up to make another joke. "Misery loves company."

I roll my eyes, but inside I'm warmed. He notices me. Me, not just Jeff's daughter, not just Carly's project. Me.

That night, I confide in Jeff about it over takeout. "Owen keeps making fun of Salinger. Says it's overrated. What do you think?"

Jeff shrugs, chopsticks poised. "Salinger makes everyone think they're the only ones who 'get it.' That's the trick. And the trap."

I grin. "You sound like Dr. Lawson."

"God forbid," he mutters, but I can tell he's secretly pleased.

Later, Bridget calls. She wants to "check in." Really, she wants intel. Her tone is cautious but insistent: "I just want to be sure you're… balanced. This whole arrangement with Jeff, it's… unconventional."

"Balanced?" I shoot back. "You mean eating vegetables? Going to class? Sleeping? Check, check, and check. Carly doesn't have to micromanage me through you, Bridget. I've got this."

There's a pause. Then, softer: "You sound different. Stronger."

"I am."

I hang up, heart hammering. Stronger. The word sticks.

I know Carly's going to be afraid of that strength. She'll try to keep me wrapped in bubble wrap. But Jeff? He just listens, really listens. He doesn't try to change my mind, doesn't scold. Sometimes he worries too much, but he never makes me feel wrong.

And that's why, when he hovers in the doorway later, asking

if I'm really okay, I surprise myself by blurting: "I think I

want to major in history. Or English. Maybe both."

He beams. "Flexing independence and picking two majors at once. That's my kid."

For once, I don't feel like I need to shrink to fit someone else's version of me.

Decisions (Jeff POV)

The loft is quiet except for the low hum of the fridge and dark except the glow of my laptop screen. Tabs sprawl across the browser like a map of my anxieties: Volvo XC40 Recharge safety ratings, IIHS crash test results, Consumer Reports reliability.

I scroll, restless. Every glossy image shows someone's daughter behind the wheel — smiling, free, alive. I try to picture Zoe there. It comes too easily. Her hair pulled back, sunlight cutting through the windshield, music blaring. Independence incarnate. And then — because I'm me — the picture fractures: headlights in the rearview, brakes failing, glass shattering.

I close my eyes. Carly's voice sneaks in, sharp and disapproving: "We can go splits on a car for graduation, Jeff. You're not doing her any favors by spoiling her. None of her suite mates have cars. Let her keep riding the train like everyone else."

This isn't spoiling. It's armor. "And she won't be in New York forever," I point out to Carly, making my insides freeze. The idea of her leaving the place where I am leads to a new idea. Where will she go after graduation? Will I follow her? Will she want me to follow her? Freedom.

And safety.

The cursor blinks in an empty dealer inquiry form. Volvo XC40 Recharge. Advanced package. My hand hovers over the keyboard. I half-smile and mutter to myself: "She'll roll her eyes at me."

But in my mind I see her laugh, see her slam the door, adjusting mirrors, about to drive into a life that terrifies me but belongs to her.

I type in my email to the dealer and hit Submit.

Secrets (Zoe POV)

The next morning, I come down the ladder and find him already in the kitchen, sleeves rolled up, coffee in hand. He looks like he hasn't slept—eyes rimmed red, jaw tight in that way it gets when he's carrying something he won't say.

"Morning," I say carefully, testing the air.

"Morning, kid." His voice is low, scratchy. He slides a mug toward me. The coffee is perfect, like always. He's meticulous about that.

I sip and study him over the rim. He doesn't meet my eyes. Memoir demons, I think. That's where my mind always goes. Pages and ghosts, keeping him up.

"You should sleep more," I tell him.

"I'll be fine," he says, too fast, the words clipped.

I let it go, but it sits with me as I take my mug to the sofa, notebook in hand. The second summer session is already kicking my ass, and still I can't stop wondering what he does at night while I'm dreaming. It's like there's a whole world he lives in that I only catch glimpses of—the late hours, the restless mornings, the faint whiff of cigarette smoke. He never mentions smoking to me, but I find the Camels in odd places.

For once, I wish he'd let me into wherever he goes.

I want to know the world you walk in when the lights go out. The one you keep locked away. You hand me fragments, but you won't hand me the whole thing. I don't know if you're protecting me or punishing me. Maybe both.

Sometimes I feel like I'm writing to you as much as I'm writing about you. Like you're a character in my essays, not a man standing in the kitchen rinsing a mug. I watch the way your shoulders tighten when you think I'm not looking. I feel like I'm learning your body language the way people learn a new language—halting, confused, but desperate to understand.

I'm hooked on The First Dead Man, but it scares me how much Blackthorn feels like Dad: the whiskey, the silence, the chasing of shadows. I find myself hoping to see Blackthorn laugh, or, God forbid, be happy for two seconds. He keeps walking, like the rain can wash guilt away. Owen says, "That's the genre. The detective isn't supposed to heal. He's supposed to endure."

I don't really understand everything that's going on, but I keep turning pages. Because here's the thing: sometimes, when Blackthorn mutters to himself about silence, about wanting someone to stay—I hear Jeff. Not Dad. Jeff. And it freaks me out.

Chapter Twenty-Four — Date Night

The Boy (Jeff POV)

The buzz comes through my phone—lobby intercom. I swipe, lift it to my ear.

"Visitor for Zoe MacKenzie." A boy's voice. English. Smooth.

My stomach drops. I don't say anything for a second too long, then: "Right. Hold on." I jab 6, unlocking the elevator.

A moment later Zoe comes down the ladder from her loft, dress swaying, arms bare, back dipping lower than I want to see. She's nervous, cheeks pink, but there's a light in her eyes.

"That's what you're wearing?" It comes out sharper than I mean.

She blinks. "What's wrong with it?"

"Nothing. I just—won't you wear a coat?"

"Dad, it's eighty degrees outside."

I stare, dumbfounded. Eighty. And she's right, of course. But still. My jaw tightens. "The skirt's short."

"It's not short!" She spins, indignant, and somehow that makes it worse. I see her not as she is, but as every man on the street will. Vulnerable. Breakable.

"I'll be fine," she says, already slipping into sandals.

Fine. The word is a blade.

I follow her out into the hallway.

The elevator dings.

Too Much Knee (Zoe POV)

I can feel his eyes on me, drilling holes in my dress, in my skin. Dad mode activated, every protective instinct blazing. My knee-length skirt is too short? Seriously?

"It's really not that short," I say again, softer this time.

He doesn't answer.

The elevator doors open, and Owen steps out, crisp and confident in a button-down. "Ready?" he asks, smiling at me, barely glancing at Jeff.

I nod, stepping past my father's storm-cloud expression. "Ready."

The silence behind me is louder than anything Owen could say.

Owen's hand brushes the small of her back as he ushers her into the elevator. Not lingering, not inappropriate, but enough to spike my pulse.

I stand rooted in the lobby, watching as she presses the button, watching as the doors slide toward each other.

"Eighty degrees," she tosses back at me with a little half-smile, as though that closes the argument.

Then the doors shut.

I'm left staring at my own reflection in the steel panel, jaw tight, pulse drumming. It feels like watching a chapter open that I didn't get to write, one where she doesn't need me to approve the outfit, or the boy, or anything.

Back inside, I pace the loft, which without her feels horribly hollow. Every sound echoes. I catch myself glancing at the clock, calculating when she'll be back. I tell myself she's fine—she's always fine. But the thought claws anyway: what if she isn't? What if he hurts her, even by accident?

I pour a glass of water, leave it untouched. Step out onto the balcony, lean against the rail, eyes on the street below. Somewhere out there, she's laughing with him. Somewhere out there, she's being seen.

And for the first time in years, I don't know if I'll be able to stand it.

The café lights are low, warm as glowing candles, bouncing off the marble counters. The Second Signal feels different tonight — the hiss of the espresso machine more subtle, the chatter replaced by a hush broken only by the scrape of chairs and the shuffle of papers. Augie has pushed the tables into loose rows, and people crowd them, notebooks open, mugs half-finished.

Owen leans toward me. "Nervous?"

I laugh, soft and shaky. "A little."

"Don't be," he says. "This is your element. Mine too. You'll see."

"You've attended these readings before, haven't you?"

"A few," he admits. "At Pendragon, I covered a few of these in the village. For the school paper."

"Pendragon?"

"The school my parents sent me to. Up in the Scottish Borders. Cold as the dickens!"

Pendragon, a word I'm definitely going to use exhaustively in my journal later. I picture to myself Owen dressed like a Knight of the Round Table, brandishing a sword.

From the Journal of Zoe Griffin MacKenzie:

He shrugs it off like it's nothing. Like everyone goes to a school like that. And I guess over there people do. 16-year-old Owen scribbling lines about old

*men with fiddles and women reading Yeats in a
draughty village hall. Of course he did. Of course
this boy who says schedule like I pronounce the
Shelley went to a school called Pendragon. I am
dying to ask him if he still has any of his school
paper writings? Does he scribble random
observations in the margins of his notebooks like I
do? Did he carry his notebooks in the open, pen or
pencil tucked behind his ear, or did he toss
everything in a bag, and walk along the rainsoaked
streets of the Hogsmeade village? I know the
village wasn't really called Hogsmeade, but the
Harry Potter books are really my only reference for
Owen's mysterious British life. Well, that and Jane
Eyre. I half expect him to drop words in casual
conversation like peat bogs, the moors, and talk
about pints and pubs.*

He strides to the front, confidence in his step like he's
been doing this all his life. He doesn't read one of the
classics — not Neruda or Frost or even Sylvia Plath. I half
expect something Byronic. He reads something of his
own, crisp lines tumbling out of him like he's spilling a
secret he doesn't mind everyone hearing. I don't
understand every word, but I feel it. His voice, his pauses,
the way he lifts his eyes and lets them land on me, just for
a beat too long.

He reads aloud from a sheet of paper in his hands:

"She walks in fragments, not in beauty—

pieces scattered like notes on a staff,

each one trembling on the edge of sound.

You think the world noisy, indifferent,

but sometimes it leans in, catches the signal,

a breath, a glance, a pulse on the wire—

and for a moment, silence learns her name."

When he finishes, the café erupts in applause, loud for such a small space. He bows, a little self-mocking, and when he sits beside me again, my pulse won't settle.

And suddenly I am nervous. Because maybe I'm not invisible anymore.

"Well?" he asks.

!!

I try to play it cool, but my voice betrays me. "You're… really good."

"Really?" His grin is boyish in a way I haven't seen.

I nod. "Really."

The night rolls on, poem after poem, but I barely hear them. Because all I can feel is the heat of him beside me, the awareness that he keeps sneaking glances like he's making sure I'm still there.

***

The crowd spills out into the street, voices lifted in laughter.

"I should probably walk you back," he says.

I shrug, teasing. "Afraid I'll get lost?"

"No." His eyes catch mine, serious now. "Afraid I'll regret it if I don't."

The city hums around us, neon and brake lights, the faint echo of a saxophone somewhere down the block. He tells me about his ambitions as a journalist. As he talks about his strategy for admission to Columbia J School, I feel acutely my own confusion about the future. What am I? A writer like Dad or a librarian like Mom? I don't see myself writing crime novels, or memoirs, or living in a loft. Yet when I speculate about the future, I come up blank. I guess that's why I can't decide on a major.

We stop under a streetlamp, the halo of light painting the pavement gold. Owen shoves his hands in his pockets, rocking on his heels like he's working up courage. We're standing in front of the Shelley, the city alive around us.

The air shifts. He steps closer, not too close, just enough.

"Zoe," he says, quiet. "Can I—?"

I don't even let him finish. I nod, heart hammering so hard I think he can hear it.

And then he leans in and kisses me.

It's simple, soft, the briefest press of lips. But it feels like the whole world rearranges in that moment, like I'm stepping into a story I didn't know I was waiting to live.

When he pulls back, I can't breathe. I don't want to.

He grins, a little sheepish now. "Sorry. That was—"

"Don't apologize," I blurt, and we both laugh, nervous and elated.

Beyond Him (Jeff POV)

I step out onto the balcony, letting the night air cool me after too many hours pacing. The city spreads below — headlights streaming, conversations rising from the street like smoke.

And then I see them.

Zoe. My Zoe. Standing under the lamplight with that boy. His shoulders angled toward her, hers tilting back, a gravity pulling them together.

I grip the railing. My breath catches.

He leans in. She doesn't flinch. She meets him there.

It's only a kiss — innocent, barely more than a brush — but it guts me. Because it's the beginning of something I can't control. A reminder that she's not just my daughter; she's a young woman, with a life beyond me, beyond the walls of this loft.

My stomach knots — pride, terror, jealousy all tangled. I want to shout, to drag her upstairs, to rewind time to when she was small enough to need me for everything. But I also want to smile, because she looks... happy. Radiant in a way I've never seen.

I step back into the loft, heart pounding. I don't know if I can survive this part of fatherhood—the part where letting go isn't a choice, it's inevitable.

She's not just mine even though I've just met her and haven't wanted to share her. I lost eighteen years but I can't stop time, or her from becoming who she's meant to be.

Trusting, Needing (Zoe POV)

I can't get the kiss out of my head. Owen asking first, so careful, like I might break if he leaned too close. The way my stomach flipped when I said yes. And then—his lips brushing mine. Quick. Sweet. Too sweet to be anything but real.

But now… he's different. Still kind, still Owen, but quieter. Careful. He jokes less, texts shorter replies. He's not avoiding me exactly, but the ease between us has been tugged, strained. And I don't know what I did wrong.

That night I find Jeff on the couch, reading glasses sliding down his nose, laptop balanced on his knees, the glow catching the salt-and-pepper in his hair. I curl up on the couch beside him. My heart beats faster. Not from nerves —okay, maybe a little—but because I've decided I have to say it.

"Dad?"

He looks over. Smiles. Wordless affection and pride and… love.

"Can I talk to you about something?" I ask, unable to keep my gaze on his.

He closes the laptop halfway, giving me his full attention. "Of course."

Curling one leg under me, I just rush it out. "It's Owen."

His face shifts, almost imperceptibly, but I notice. Of course I notice.

I push forward. "He kissed me."

Jeff stays silent, waiting.

"I liked it. A lot." The words come out like a confession. "But now he's acting different. Like maybe he regrets it. Or maybe I should."

Jeff leans back, rubbing his chin. "Did he push you?"

"No." My voice is sharp. "He asked. I said yes."

"Then don't regret it." He says it simply, like it's the most obvious truth in the world. "If he's pulling back, that's his stuff. Not yours."

I stare at him, trying to read the lines on his face. For a second I think I see something else—but it's gone before I can name it.

"Thanks," I say finally, and stand, retreating toward the ladder. "Goodnight."

"Goodnight, Zo," he says softly.

Up in my loft, I fall onto the bed but don't sleep. My lips still feel the ghost of Owen's kiss, and now my father's voice, steady and sure, is tangled up in it.

Party Invitations (Jeff POV)

I'm still on the couch, staring at the closed laptop, when the phone rings. Bridget.

"Have you locked in the rooftop garden?" she asks. Straight to business.

"I'll handle it," I say.

"Good. Keep her in the dark." Click. She's gone.

I toss the phone onto the table and rub my eyes. Keep Zoe in the dark. That phrase hits harder than Bridget realizes. What Zoe confessed to me just before the call is still echoing. She came to me. She trusted me with something that embarrassed her, something she didn't have to share with her dad. But she did. She came to me. Because she knows I'll tell her the truth—not wall her off, not keep her in the dark.

I close the laptop, but I don't move. I picture Zoe bent over her textbooks, Owen Aubrey's name floating around her orbit, Carly and Bridget scheming. I need to do more than sit here.

The car's already decided. She deserves safety, independence. Carly and Bridget can fight me, but I'm not budging.

And the guest list—mine. If we're celebrating her, we're doing it right. Owen Aubrey. Augie from Second Signal. Dr. Lawson, who she trusts more than anyone. People who matter to her.

I make a note to myself: call them. Every one.

Because this party isn't theirs. It's Zoe's.

***

Invitations (Jeff POV)

I start the morning with the easy ones.

Augie picks up on the second ring, his voice warm with that southern drawl.

"It's Jeff Griffin. Zoe's father."

"I know who you are," he says with a chuckle.

"I'm throwing her a surprise party. Rooftop, here at the loft, the Shelley on Spring Street. She thinks it's just family, but I want the people who've really been there for her in New York to show up. You, especially."

"I'll be there," Augie says simply. "Wouldn't miss it. She's a good kid. And she'll need someone to smuggle in decent coffee."

Dr. Lawson is brisk when she answers.

"Professor Lawson, this is Jeff Griffin."

"Well, well, well! The Jeff Griffin." Her tone is wry. "To what do I owe this honor?"

"Nothing. You flatter me."

"I do, but it's no less than the father of a delightful girl deserves."

"Speaking of…I'm hosting a party for her birthday. A surprise. She talks about you more than anyone else at school, so—well—I'd be grateful if you came."

Silence. Then her voice softens. "If Zoe wants me there, I'll be there."

Owen is the toughest. His card sits on my desk all morning before I finally dial.

"Hello?"

"Jeff Griffin here. Zoe's father."

A beat. Then: "Yes, sir."

"She's having a birthday. A surprise party. Intimate family, friends. Rooftop here at the loft. The Shelley, Spring Street. Consider this an official invitation."

His voice cracks slightly. "Thank you. I'll be there."

"Owen?"

"Sir?"

"Don't make me regret it."

I can hear the intake of breath and I almost feel sorry for him. What can I say? Fathers are only human.

Later, I send the generals a group text—Bridget, Carly.

For Zoe's party: I've invited a few others who matter to her. Dr. Lawson, her professor. Augie from the café. Owen, her friend from the Herald.

The dots bubble on my screen. Bridget replies first:

Professor? Cafe person? Who's Owen?

Then Carly:

Owen, the boyfriend?

I type back, slow, deliberate:

Yes. They're important to Zoe. That's all that matters.

Worries (Zoe POV)

From the Journal of Zoe Griffin MacKenzie:

I texted Owen. No reply yet. Dad—brooding all the time. Frowning. The crease on his forehead. Bridget's interference. Carly's shadow. They're planning something. Everything feels different since the kiss. No one tells me anything. I was visible for two seconds at the poetry reading, when Owen kissed me. I wish he would text me back. I've been reading The First Dead Man again and I have questions about tropes, something he knows a lot about. There's this whole femme fatale thing in the book. There's this femme fatale named Harley who Blackthorn spars with. It's sort of like Sherlock Holmes and Irene Adler; that's what it reminds me of anyway. Not that I'm well-versed in Conan Doyle, but I did watch the BBC's Sherlock series, so I know the basics.

So far I've skimmed the Harley scenes. Not because they're badly written—they're too good, actually. The way she walks into a room and every man goes blind, the way her laugh feels like a blade. It makes me queasy, like I'm trespassing into some place I don't want to go.

Isn't this the anti-feminist thing Owen would lecture me about? I'd ask him, but he's still ghosting me. So instead I skim. Pretend I didn't see it. Pretend it's just another trope, another trench coat in a rainy alley.

Because if I look too close, I'll start wondering who she really is. And I'm not ready for that.

Chapter Twenty-Five — Daughters

His Own First Kiss (Jeff POV)

The loft is hushed except for the tap of the keys on my MacBook. Zoe's curled up in the nook upstairs, the faint rhythm of her sleep-breath drifting down through the rafters. I should quit, should turn in, but the memoir won't leave me alone.

I stare at what I've typed, at the blinking cursor:

> *First kiss, age 13. A football game at St. John's, Baton Rouge. Becky Morris behind the bleachers. She leaned in quickly, a peck that startled me, and when I leaned in for another she pulled away like I'd broken some rule I didn't know. I spent weeks replaying it, convinced I'd done it wrong. Too fast. Too awkward. Too me.*

> *I couldn't ask anyone—what boy admits he can't kiss? So I turned to movies. Rented anything with a romance subplot, studied the angles and timing like it was homework, the way hands were supposed to cup cheeks, the way lips were supposed to linger. Not because I was some young Casanova*

I rub my temple, thinking of Zoe's first kiss, the way Owen's hand hovered before it landed, the way she lit up even through her nerves. Brave in ways I wasn't. And I wonder if she'll replay that kiss the way I did, second-guessing, over-analyzing, searching for cues.

I type out one more line:

Maybe the first kiss is meant to be imperfect. Proof you're learning, proof you're alive.

My phone buzzes, screen lighting up with Theo's name. FaceTime. I swipe and his face fills the screen, the hospital chaos spilling in around him. He signs quickly, urgent: [Julia's water broke. St. Luke's. Now.]

Adrenaline jolts me upright. "On our way."

I shove the notebook aside and call up to the nook: "Zo! Get dressed. Hospital. It's time."

She's awake instantly—scrambling down the ladder, hair wild, eyes wide. "The baby?"

I nod, already grabbing the keys to the bike. "The baby."

Within minutes we're straddling the bike, helmets snapped, the garage doors rising like a curtain. Now we're thundering into the night, the city opening in front of us, the signal pulling us forward. I gun the throttle and we surge into the New York night. Wind slaps my face, but it feels like breath, like motion itself is oxygen. Zoe holds tight, arms locked at my ribs, her heartbeat pounding through my back.

The city blurs past—red taillights smearing, bridges humming under our tires, skyline cut sharp against the dark. Sirens wail somewhere else, in another direction. Our lane clears like the road knows where we're headed.

I lean us into the curve, the East River glinting beside us, and shout over the wind: "We're coming!"

Her grip tightens. The buildings rise. The hospital looms ahead, its lights like a beacon.

Newborn (Zoe POV)

The hospital hums with fluorescent light and muted footsteps. We ride the elevator up, the two of us pressed into opposite corners, his leather jacket still carrying the sharp scent of the night ride. Neither of us says much. What is there to say? Julia's labor is hours ahead of us, and we're not family—not officially. We're just the ones Theo waved in with a look that said 'don't leave me alone in this.'

The waiting room is beige, tired, too warm. Jeff sinks into a chair, stretching his long legs, tapping his fingers against his thigh like he wants a cigarette but knows better. I sit across from him, pretending to scroll my phone, but really just studying him. He looks like he's bracing against something, but not the birth. Something deeper.

He catches me staring, and for a second the edge softens. "Takes forever," he mutters. "Hospitals."

I shrug. "Ethan's bar mitzvah felt longer."

He almost laughs. Almost. Then silence returns, comfortable for a beat, then too sharp again.

I want to tell him about the insight I had last night, reading The First Dead Man, but of course I can't tell him, since I haven't decided whether to tell him I'm reading that book. I honestly don't know that he'll be pleased.

I shouldn't have read this before bed. Blackthorn hears a baby crying and thinks only of endings. Of wreckage. Of despair. My dad—because it is him, no matter how he hides under Blackthorn's trench coat—wrote this. And here I am, his baby, now almost grown, reading how he believed newborn life was just meat for the grinder. It stings. I don't want to believe he thought that way when I was born, but maybe he did. What saves me, what keeps me from slamming the book shut, is the flicker at the end. He doesn't call it hope—of course he doesn't, he'd choke on the word—but it's there anyway. A spark he can't name, but I can. Me.

I want to tell him that. That maybe Blackthorn was wrong, but Jeff Griffin—my dad—doesn't have to be.

Hours fold over. A nurse comes and goes. At one point Jeff buys me a Sprite from the vending machine, presses it into my hand without a word.

When the door finally opens and Theo steps out, he's beaming, sweat still on his forehead. He signs before he even speaks, hands flying with joy. [Julia's resting. The baby's here. A girl.]

"Name?" Jeff asks, voice lower than usual, like he's afraid to break the air.

Theo signs again, slower this time. [Julia picked it. Elise Aurora Arceneaux.]

The name lands in me like light cracking a window. Elise Aurora. Something about it feels like the promise of morning.

Through the nursery glass, we see her. Tiny, impossibly so, swaddled in pink, her fists jerking in random bursts of motion. Theo steps inside, and when he lifts her, his whole body sags as if under the weight of the emotion.

Jeff stands close enough that our shoulders brush. His gray eyes don't leave the glass. And when Theo turns the baby just enough so we both catch her profile, Jeff exhales like he's been holding his breath for years.

Vital Record (Jeff POV)

Atlanta. Bureau of Vital Records. August 3, 2006.

When the envelope came, I tore it open like it might still be warm. Father: unknown. Weight: 5 pounds, 12 ounces.

Length: 19 inches. Paper proof of what I should have known all along.

I wrote Blackthorn into corners I couldn't get out of. Men who saw new life only as another liability, another mouth to feed in a world already bleeding. I made him cradle despair like a cigarette stub, smoldering down to ash.

But the truth is, even then—even at my worst—I knew that wasn't the whole story. Despair is easy; it writes itself. What's harder is admitting you kept writing because something in you wanted to be wrong. That maybe, just maybe, there was a flicker at the end of the alley, a light you didn't deserve but couldn't stop imagining.

I never named it. Couldn't. But I kept chasing it anyway.

Beautiful (Zoe POV)

I don't know what memory just cut through him, but when he straightens, I can feel the weight settle back into his frame. He presses his knuckles lightly against the glass. "Beautiful," he whispers.

I nod. My throat's too tight to answer. Dad is shining through the static.

Chapter Twenty-Six — Suspicions

The city's still blue when we step out of the sliding doors. The automatic hiss behind us sounds like a held breath finally letting go. I hand Zoe the helmet and watch her braid disappear under it; she tightens the strap like she's been doing it her whole life.

The Ducati coughs awake. We roll out beneath the sodium lights, the concrete slick with that hospital-night sheen. When we hit the open street she finds my ribs with both arms and holds—not tentative, not afraid—just there, like an answer I can feel.

We move through pockets of silence: a bakery truck yawning itself into gear; a man with a hose waking the sidewalk; a dark bus lurching empty toward a terminal. Traffic lights blink their lonely metronome. I keep us in that thin seam where New York hasn't decided what it is yet.

Her helmet rests between my shoulder blades. Every time I shift, she shifts, a small counterweight that makes the bike feel steadier than it should. I think of Theo's face —joy cracked wide open—and Julia's tired smile, and the new name that's going to change their house forever. I let it wash through me and try not to think about everything I can't get back.

We catch a green river of lights and thread south, the wind cold enough to clear the fog of fluorescent hours. A gull slices the dawn above the water. Somewhere to our left the city exhales steam like a sleeping animal. I lean us into a long, empty curve and feel her grip tighten, then ease, like trust learning the shape of itself.

"Breakfast?" I call when we coast to a red and the world finally offers up a little noise. The visor lifts; I hear her laugh, small and hoarse from the night.

"Only if they have pancakes," she says.

"They all have pancakes."

The light flips. We slide through the last of the blue and into the first pale gold. I take the long way toward SoHo on purpose, chasing quiet streets, chasing time. The day is coming whether we invite it or not. For another few minutes, it's just the two of us inside an empty city that doesn't know our names.

I turn toward a diner that opens before sunrise, the kind with chrome trim and blue booths and a waitress who calls everybody honey. We idle to the curb. Zoe hops off, pulls the helmet free, and shakes her hair loose. For a second she looks at me like she's seeing something settle in my face, and whatever it is, it doesn't scare her.

"Pancakes," she reminds me.

"Stack as high as you can stand," I say, and kill the engine.

She laughs, tired but real, and that's good enough for me.

Inside, the place smells like coffee and syrup. Vinyl booths, cracked menus, waitresses who've been here since forever. We slide into a booth, helmets piled by the window. She orders chocolate chip pancakes without hesitation. I go with black coffee and eggs, more out of habit than appetite.

Zoe pours syrup over her stack, humming under her breath. I watch her for a moment, the light catching the tired pride in her face, and feel something unclench in me. She belongs here. With me.

Halfway through her stack of pancakes, my phone buzzes on the table. I glance at the screen. A New York number I recognize—the Volvo dealer. I grimace, and push it aside. I hit ignore and flip the phone face-down.

She notices, but doesn't ask. Instead she nudges my plate with her fork. "You gonna finish that?"

I slide the last strip of bacon across to her. "Happy now?"

She grins around the bite. "For the moment."

"Who was that?" she asks, mouth full of chocolate and doubt.

"Nothing urgent," I deflect, stirring my coffee.

She squints. "Uh-huh."

I change the subject, asking about the Arceneaux baby instead. It works—her whole face lights up as she mimics Theo's signing through tears, telling me again how Elise Aurora looked so small and yet so infinite at once. I let her talk. Some things can wait.

The Parking Space (Zoe POV)

By the time we step out into the brightening morning, I'm sticky with syrup and wide awake despite myself. Dad looks like he hasn't slept in days, but there's a strange energy about him—lighter, almost.

The bike rumbles us into the underground garage. I slide off first, tugging off the helmet, stretching stiff legs. That's when I notice it: a new parking space, right next to his. Fresh paint, same number: 5A.

I blink. "Wait. Since when are there two five-As?"

He hesitates just a second too long. "Oh. That. I, uh, bought an extra spot. Figured maybe I'd get a car. You know—something boring. A vehicle adults drive. A dad car." He gestures vaguely at the Ducati, like that explains anything. "Not just a tortured-artist death trap."

Shock rattles me. "You're getting rid of the bike?"

"Maybe." He shrugs, trying to play it off.

I hate the thought of it. "Well—can I have it then?" The words spill before I think.

He actually chokes out a laugh. "Um, Zoe, have you ever driven a motorcycle?"

I cross my arms. "Not yet."

He shakes his head, amused and horrified all at once. "Trust me, this isn't exactly a beginner's bike. Too much power, not enough mercy. If you want to break every bone in your body, sure, I'll hand over the keys. Otherwise? No."

I roll my eyes, but inside, I'm warmed by it. The banter, the ridiculousness—it feels like ours.

We step into the elevator, doors sliding closed, carrying us back up into the loft, back into our little world.

Chapter Twenty-Seven — Final Birthday Plans

Pins & Needles (Jeff POV)

The elevator doors open, and Zoe darts past me, kicking off her sneakers. She drops her bag by the sofa, then wanders toward the piano like it pulls her on invisible strings. Her fingers find Schubert almost before she sits, the same Impromptus she's been playing all summer. Smooth, practiced, safe.

I stand by the counter, setting my helmet down, pretending to flip through yesterday's mail. But I know the difference. She used to vanish up to Bronxville to practice on campus; lately she stays here, playing only when I'm out. And when I catch her at the piano, it's always Schubert, never anything new.

She's hiding something. I can feel it in the way her shoulders tense when I walk by.

I head for the fridge, grab a bottle of water, and lean against the counter. "Sounds good, Zo."

"Thanks." She doesn't look up, eyes locked on the keys.

It's her birthday in a few days. The rooftop is nearly ready —tables rented, lights strung, cake ordered. I've invited everyone who matters: Theo, Julia, and baby Elise; her Baton Rouge clan—Nancy and Cole and my nephews, Bridget and Ed and their son, Ethan, and Carly. My additions—Augie, Dr. Lawson, Owen—are raising eyebrows, but damn it, they're important to her.

And then there's the Volvo. Parked at Theo's for safekeeping. Silver-gray, pristine, hers. The key fob locked in my safe along with the Memoir fragments. I can barely keep the lie straight when she glances at me sideways, suspicion flickering.

She finishes the piece and lets her hands fall to her lap. "You've been out a lot lately," she says softly.

"Party prep." I smile, easy as I can manage. "Nothing sinister."

She knows we're doing something for her birthday, that the Baton Rouge clan is coming up, but she thinks it's just a dinner. She has no idea she's getting a catered rooftop party with live music. Augie arranged for a band he knows, who sometimes play at the Second Signal, to do the music. I've made sure they know all of Zoe's favorite songs.

Her eyes narrow, but she lets it go, rising from the bench. "I'm going to shower."

I nod, waiting until the bathroom door clicks shut before exhaling. The truth presses against my ribs, but tomorrow, she'll know.

Tomorrow, the signal has to come through, loud and clear.

Feeling Invisible Again (Zoe POV)

He's out, the loft is mine, and the piano is a living thing waiting to breathe. I slide the fallboard back, touch middle C, and the sound settles me like a hand between my shoulder blades. I warm up with scales until my brain quiets. Then Schubert—always Schubert—because it keeps my heart from trying to sprint.

I switch to the pages in the old book that was his dad's—pencil edits, crossings-out, rebuilt measures that feel like someone arguing their way toward grace. I don't know if I'll play it tomorrow; the thought of performing in front of everyone makes my stomach flip. But practicing it makes me feel closer to him and to the man before him. A line.

When my phone finally buzzes, I'm disappointed it's not Owen.

Bridget: Landing at 11. Picking up Carly. Nancy's already in the city. We'll come by at noon and take you dress shopping. Bring comfortable shoes.

My pulse ticks up. The Generals. I put the fallboard down slowly like I'm calming a skittish animal.

***

The water steams around me, fogging the mirror, but it doesn't clear my head. Owen hasn't answered my last two texts. He answered one this morning—short, clipped, like he was in a rush. Busy. Talk later.

Later never comes.

I lean against the tile, listening to the rush of water drown out the Schubert still echoing in my ears. I should've stopped playing sooner. Jeff noticed. He always notices. The thing is—I want him to notice, just not yet. Not until I can play it perfectly, not until it's ready.

The secret burns in my chest. And Owen's silence twists it tighter.

I step out, pull on pajamas, and pad barefoot through the loft. Jeff is at the counter, laptop open, but when he sees me he shuts the screen like I caught him in something.

"Nothing's wrong," I say before he can ask. My voice is too quick, too sharp. "I'm just trying to perfect this piece. That's all."

He studies me with those gray eyes, steady and searching. I walk past before he can pin me there.

Subtle Signals (Jeff POV)

She's lying. I know it. Not in a dangerous way—just the kind of lie kids tell when they want space. Still, it eats at me. I want to tell her everything—the car, the rooftop, how I've planned it down to the last lightbulb. But if I do, I ruin the surprise.

And I want this to be hers. A moment no one can take away.

I used to tell my parents I was volunteering as a yearbook staffer. Truth was, the yearbook staff only met once a month, and most of the time we didn't do much beyond arguing about fonts. But "yearbook" sounded wholesome, responsible, the kind of thing that made Mom nod with approval and Dad stop asking questions. Where was I for real? Coffee Call, sometimes. Powdered sugar thick in the air, beignets stacked on the tray between me and whoever I was trying to impress that week. Girls from the "sister school" or once even a freshmen at LSU who thought I was older than I was. It wasn't the girls so much as the freedom, the way the lie carved out a little pocket of space that was mine. My parents thought I was editing layouts under fluorescent lights. In truth I was learning the art of pretending that I had my own life.

It wasn't rebellion, not really. It was wanting space. A little privacy. A corner of the world that was mine alone. I see it now in Zoe's music. The Schubert looping when I walk in, the way she insists she's just practicing. Maybe she is. Maybe she isn't. Either way, I know what it means. She wants her corner. And the best thing I can do is let her have it.

I close the laptop and glance toward the piano. Tomorrow she'll play something different—I can feel it. She's hiding a gift (?) the way I'm hiding mine. And maybe that's fair. Maybe that's how we both survive each other: secrets now, truth later.

I sip my water and let her retreat upstairs.

Shadows (Zoe POV)

I curl up on my bed in the loft-within-the-loft, phone in hand. No new messages. I almost type — 'Are you mad at me?' — but delete it. If Owen's pulling back, maybe I scared him. Maybe the kiss was too much.

Maybe I'm too much.

My thumb hovers over Jeff's contact. He'd tell me not to spiral, but I can't bring myself to ask. He's hiding things too. I can feel it. Whatever this is between us—it's not as simple as "father" and "daughter." It's light, yes, but shadows still press in around the edges.

I tuck the phone under my pillow. Tomorrow is my birthday. Tomorrow, maybe, things will shift again.

Loud Silence (Jeff POV)

The Volvo key fob stays in the safe. Always.

I put it there the day the dealer handed it over, tucked inside the black folder with the owner's manual and registration papers. Out of sight, out of reach.

I know Zoe. One glimpse of that shiny silver emblem and she'd sniff me out like a bloodhound. I'm not careless enough to leave it lying around on the counter or rattling in my pocket. Not when I've managed to keep the whole ordeal of ordering, insuring, and even registering the damn car under wraps.

For now, the Volvo sits in Theo's driveway in Forest Hills, looking out of place among the neighbor's battered minivans. He teases me about it every time I come by — signing, [you know you're basically playing Santa Claus in August, right?] — but he keeps the secret.

So when Zoe looks at me with that suspicious tilt of her head, I just grin and offer to make waffles. It buys me time. Long enough to pull this off.

But keeping secrets gnaws at me. It feels too close to the old habits — the silence, the omissions, the half-truths that got me here in the first place. I tell myself this is different. This is joy deferred, not truth withheld. Still, it's a thin line, and I can feel myself wobbling on it.

She thinks I'm distracted because of the memoir. Or because Carly won't leave me alone. Both are true. But the truth humming underneath it all is parked in Forest Hills, gleaming under the summer sun, waiting for her.

***

I'm up early, coffee in hand, pacing my own roof like a contractor I didn't hire. String lights: tested. Planters: watered. The super okayed the extra tables and the rental chairs, and I've got a florist bringing a few low arrangements so the skyline still does the heavy lifting. I text Theo a thank-you for babysitting a very conspicuous secret in his driveway.

> Me: She's gonna love it.

> Theo: (picture of a blue metallic ribbon on Zoe's present) JULIA PICKED THE COLOR. NO CHANGING IT.

Downstairs, I crack the safe and tuck the key fob back inside, far in the corner behind tax folders and a box of old photos. No "accidental" discoveries. The second spot in the garage—fresh paint still bright—waits like a promise: 5A. Twin 5A spots. Mine and hers. Every time I think about rolling the Volvo in there, I almost blow my cover.

Invites: I fire off the last three.

—Dr. Lawson, because Zoe lights up when she says her name.

—Augie at Second Signal Café, because he's been quietly looking out for my kid.

—Owen Aubrey, because… because he matters to her.

I keep my message simple: Rooftop on the 3rd at 7. Don't tell her. Dress code: whatever won't make an old man feel ancient.

I leave a note on the piano: *Running errands. Back by 2. Play as loud as you want.* If she's going to practice, I want her to feel the place responding to her, not to me hovering. I grab my keys. In the hallway, I glance at the door marked 5B, the vacancy where no neighbor exists, and let my imagination run for a second—two lofts, the whole floor, fewer ways for anyone to hurt her. I shake it off. One miracle at a time.

The Generals (Jeff POV)

At noon my loft looks like a staging area: spare chairs, a box of bamboo plates, votives. I barely have time to shove the box under the counter before the elevator dings and they sweep in.

Bridget first—crisp, composed, already scanning. Carly next—contained, assessing. Nancy last, sunglasses perched on her head like a crown she didn't have to buy.

"Where does Zoe sleep?" Carly asks, peering upward toward the ladder.

"The loft," I say. "Her loft." I gesture, and there's no way to keep the pride out of my voice.

Carly's eye flicks over the piano, the desk, the typewriter, like she's building a case. Bridget's neutral; she's saving her verdict for later. Nancy takes one long, satisfied look and nods once, like a general who just inspected a winning position.

Zoe comes down the ladder, braid loosening, face fresh and careful. Nancy opens her arms. "Hello, birthday girl in progress."

"I'm not the birthday girl," Zoe says, deadpan.

"Technicality," Nancy replies, kissing her cheek. Then to me, with mock sternness: "We're borrowing your child."

"Permission granted," I say. Zoe shoots me a pained look before being swept between them like a diplomatic convoy. When the door shuts behind them, the loft exhales. I do, too.

Mannequin (Zoe POV)

SoHo is a shimmering heat mirage and the sidewalks are theater. Nancy votes couture. Bridget says Bloomingdale's. Carly says, "There's a Jersey mall with—"

"We are not going to New Jersey," Nancy says, and it's so definitive that I want to applaud.

Bloomingdale's, then. The escalators hum, the sales associates pounce, and Carly starts a gentle flanking maneuver: "Maybe something structured. Classic. Conservative."

The floor tilts. My breaths go shallow. Hello, panic. I name it, like Dr. Patel taught me. I let my attention drop into my feet. Weight over heels. Four corners of the breath. In—two—three—four. Hold. Out—two—three—four.

"Try this," Nancy says, holding up a dress that is somehow simple and beautiful at once—slate blue, cap sleeves, a clean line that looks like it belongs to me. "We're not turning you into someone you don't recognize."

In the dressing room, I smooth the fabric down my sides and stare at the mirror until my face stops buzzing. I step out. For a second three different versions of my life are reflected in the panel of glass across from us.

Bridget presses two fingers to her lips. "Perfect."

Carly hesitates, then nods, unwilling to be the only holdout. "The color's...nice."

Nancy beams. "That's a yes from all judges."

At lunch—some overpriced bistro that smells like melted butter—Bridget orders salads for all of us before I can speak. I don't mind; eating and talking at the same time with three generals is a tactical error.

"How's the summer going?" Bridget asks, neutral.

"Good," I say. "Classes are almost done. I like my professors."

Carly cuts in, voice soft but honed. "Are you taking your medication on schedule?"

Nancy puts down her fork. "Carly."

"It's a question, not a prosecution."

"It sounds like prosecution."

I feel the old tightening, the urge to disappear. I find the spoon, trace its edge. Feet. Chair. Breath. I answer calmly. "Yes. On schedule."

Carly opens her mouth again. Nancy's look could level a building. Bridget steps in. "We're proud of how you're handling the load," she says, eyes steady on mine. "Truly."

Just like that, some internal knot loosens. Nancy squeezes my knee under the table. We talk about nothing for a while—Ethan's latest obsession, the humidity, whether slate blue is a "fall" color or if that's just nonsense. I breathe. I survive. I choose.

Afterward, Nancy hails a cab like she's commanding cavalry. "My work here is done," she tells me with a sly smile. "Don't let them make you buy shoes you can't walk in."

Bridget laughs; Carly pretends to. We break apart at the curb, and for the first time all day, I'm not bracing for impact.

Mission Accomplished (Jeff POV)

They return in shifts: first Nancy to drop off a garment bag and whisper "it's good" before vanishing toward Midtown; then Bridget and Carly with tissue-papered boxes and an air of satisfied fatigue.

"How's it looking?" I ask, calling from the kitchen, where I've been chopping things for a stew.

"Handled," Bridget says, which in Bridget means approved.

Carly glances at me at work in the kitchen. "You cook?" She says it like it's a riddle she can't solve.

"Sometimes," I say. "More lately."

Zoe meets my eyes over their shoulders. There's a tiny flare of relief there, like she's stepping off a moving train and found solid ground. I want to say 'I see you, you're great, you don't have to do it alone anymore.' Instead, I lift the garment bag like it's precious cargo and hang it where nothing can touch it.

When the door finally closes and the loft belongs to us again, I exhale. "Tomorrow," I say.

"Tomorrow," she echoes, and for once, the word feels like a promise instead of a cliff.

Resolve (Zoe POV)

He disappears onto the roof to check lights "one more time," and I sit at the piano with the new dress hanging like a moon in the corner of my eye. I try Schubert again. My hands are steadier now. My breathing is, too.

I text Owen one more time.

Me: last chance to tell me you're not ghosting me

Three dots. Then nothing. I laugh—half-annoyed, half-fond—and let it go. The left hand picks up a pattern; the right hand answers. I'm not practicing for a performance. I'm practicing for me, for tomorrow, for the person I'm still figuring out how to be.

Jeff comes back down, cheeks wind-pink from the roof. "Everything okay?" he asks.

"Yeah," I say, and I mean it. "Everything's okay."

Chapter Twenty-Eight — Calm Before the Storm

Simple Things (Jeff POV)

The knife moves easy in my hand as I rock it through carrots, celery, onions. Zoe is beside me at the counter, tearing basil leaves and humming something under her breath. A stew for later—it's been forever since I bothered making one. Feels different now, more deliberate, almost domestic.

"Carly accused you of not feeding me," she says suddenly, tone light, but I hear the barb under it.

I glance up. "Yeah? And what did you say?"

She smirks. "I didn't have to. Nancy nearly knocked her out."

I laugh—can't help it—and shake my head. "Classic Nancy."

"Honestly, I thought I'd have to drag her off Carly by the hair," she says, almost giddy at the memory. Then her expression softens. "It was nice, though. To have someone in my corner."

"You've always had someone in your corner," I say, a little too quickly. She tilts her head at me, not letting me off easy, and I turn back to the onions before she can see too much on my face.

By the time the vegetables are chopped and tucked into the pot, the light outside has gone from pale afternoon to that honey-colored early evening. She tugs me toward the balcony like it's the most natural thing in the world.

Games (Zoe POV)

We sprawl in the chaise lounges, city buzzing underneath us, the sky washed with faint streaks of pink. No stars—never stars—but I don't care. It's peaceful.

"You ever play chess?" he asks, holding up the set he's dug out from a shelf.

"A little," I say. "Prepare to lose."

He raises an eyebrow but sets the board between us. The game goes slowly, full of smack talk and laughter, and when I finally corner his king, he groans like I just stole the Nobel Prize.

"Rematch tomorrow," he says.

"Fine. You'll lose again."

The pieces are still scattered on the board when I lean back, arms folded behind my head. Something inside me loosens, and before I know it, stories are spilling out.

"Bridget used to play cards with me at the kitchen table," I
say. "Rummy, mostly. She'd let me win half the time. Ethan
learned quick though—he started beating us both."

He smiles, listening. Really listening.

"I taught Ethan to swim once. Or tried. He screamed
bloody murder when his face hit the water, but then he
finally paddled across, and I swear Bridget cried harder
than he did."

I pause, catching his expression, soft as candlelight, and I
keep going. "One Thanksgiving, I tripped carrying gravy
and dumped it all over my dress. Carly didn't even yell—
she just sighed, like, 'of course it's Zoe.'"

His jaw clenches at that, but I hurry on.

"Carly once wanted me to do this mother-daughter
fashion show fundraiser for the library. Matching dresses,
the whole nine yards. I was fourteen and dying of
embarrassment. I called Nana in Atlanta and begged her
to save me. She threatened to tell everyone what
happened on prom night 2001 if Carly didn't drop it."

He whistles low. "Prom night 2001?"

I shrug. "Still don't know what that was about. But Carly
panicked. Dropped the idea immediately."

We both fall quiet, the city humming below.

Her Fragments (Jeff POV)

She's stretched out beside me, hair spilling over the
lounge cushion, telling stories like she's offering me

pieces of herself. I want to freeze the moment, to hold on to this lightness before it all slips back into shadows.

"Sounds like Nana knew how to handle Carly," I murmur.

"Yeah," she says softly. "Sometimes I think she's the only one who ever really did."

We sit like that, shoulder to shoulder, letting the evening roll in. And for once, there's no panic clinging to her, no storm on the edge of breaking. Just Zoe. Just my daughter. And me, not screwing it up.

Chapter Twenty-Nine — Party Prep

Makeover (Zoe POV)

I'm trapped in a chair like a doll, three pairs of hands circling me like hawks. Nancy is sweeping a makeup brush over my face.

"Tilt your chin," she commands. "No, not like you're in a mugshot. Up. Poise. Pretend you're on the cover of Vogue."

"Vogue?" I mutter. "For a family birthday dinner?"

"You only turn 19 once, sweetheart." Oh, great. Now she's uncorking the mascara.

"Wait," I protest, leaning back slightly. "Mascara? Really? I'd rather not."

She ignores me and expertly coats my eyelashes. Carly is fussing with braids. In trying not to be too rough—her usual mistake—she overcorrects, her movements so careful they almost hurt.

"Is that too tight?" she keeps asking, like she's afraid a real tug will shatter me.

"It's fine," I say, even though it's far from fine.

"Geesh, Carly, she's not made of glass," Bridget says. She swoops in with the curling iron, her efficiency a sharp contrast. "Hold still, Zoe, just one more pass on this side, then you'll be finished."

Carly clips and pins. They bicker, but not about Jeff, not anymore.

"Don't pull so tight," Carly mutters.

"I'm not pulling tight at all," Bridget counters.

"Three women, one girl's head," Nancy sighs, lifting a lipstick like a sword. "No pain, no gain, Carly. Pucker up, Zoe."

I can't help smiling. Jeff's writing nook has been converted into their makeshift salon. His desk lamp turned into my mirror light.

"You look like your father when you frown," Bridget observes.

Carly tilts her head, unable to argue, though clearly wanting to. "Better cheekbones."

"Thanks," I say drily.

"You look beautiful," Carly says softly, leaning close so our reflections frame us both.

Bridget plants a hand on each of our shoulders. "She looks polished but still 19. Not overdone."

"Absolutely not," Nancy agrees. "She's a Griffin through and through."

Carly flinches. "Half," she mutters. "She's half Griffin."

The room stills. Bridget's eyes flash. But Nancy only shrugs. "Half, whole, whatever math you do, she's still ours."

Something shifts in my chest. Carly conceding, even halfway, feels enormous. She's not fighting it. She's sharing. For once, I'm not mascara-proof.

I slip away to my nook to pull on the dress—blue, simple, mine.

The women clear away the arsenal of brushes and pins. They file upstairs to the rooftop, leaving me a moment of quiet.

Reflections (Jeff POV)

The Shelley rooftop garden glows with string lights I hung myself, buzzing faintly against the darkening sky. Echo Union, Augie's favorite band to hire for events at the Second Signal, is tuning up in the corner, drumsticks clicking, the singer testing her mic with a low hum. The city spreads around us, restless, alive, but here it feels contained—ours.

I lean on the railing, watching the skyline catch fire with the last streaks of sunset. My mind drifts, as it always does on this day.

August 3, 2006. I was 22. A year out of college, sweating through a fifth-floor walk-up with no air-conditioning. My desk was a slab of wood I'd hauled off the curb, my chair wobbled every time I shifted. I lived on bagels that went stale in a day and cheap cigarettes. That morning I sat in front of a blinking cursor, telling myself I was a writer, though I had nothing to show for it.

And while I sat there, Zoe MacKenzie was born—miles away in Atlanta. My daughter. The word didn't exist in my life yet. I didn't hear the signal break through. I didn't feel the earth tilt. I just cursed the heat and tried to fill the page. She took her first breath, and I took another drag off a cigarette. Twenty-two years old, and I had no idea the most important person in my life had just entered the world.

Even now, I can't picture it. The hospital, the crib, Bridget hovering nearby—it's blank space. Maybe that's why it eats at me. One day I'll have to force Carly to hand over Zoe's baby book, the photographs, anything to stitch those hours into my memory. Right now, all I have is absence.

The roof door opens. Nancy, Carly, Bridget step out, surveying the space like generals. Behind them: Julia, glowing with baby Elise in her arms; Theo holding the carrier; Cole and the boys trailing in after an afternoon on the boats in Central Park. Ed and Ethan arrive fresh from the museums, their bags still slung over their shoulders.

Augie and Dr. Lawson step out of the elevator together, bickering amiably about music. Owen lingers at the edge, awkward but trying not to look it.

Everyone's here. Everyone but her.

My chest tightens, the same way it did stringing these lights, arranging these tables, setting the candles. Every detail has been for her.

Chapter Thirty — The Toast

Waiting (Jeff POV)

My nerves are ticking in my chest. Lights are strung overhead, the band Echo Union tuning up in the corner, the tables dressed and waiting.

Everyone gathers, voices low and expectant, the band keeping their chords soft. I check my watch. Time.

I slip toward the elevator, straighten my collar, and wait for the elevator to open.

I travel down to the fifth floor.

Surprise (Zoe POV)

Jeff is beside me in the hallway. As we enter the elevator, my dress swishes against my knees, my hair pinned and braided in ways that still feel like other people's hands on me. He looks at me once, searching, like he wants to say something, but doesn't. The elevator hums, rising.

When the doors open—chaos.

"SURPRISE!"

Lights flare, voices crash together, and I flinch back before I realize they're all smiling, all looking at me. A wall of faces—family, strangers, almost-strangers—all here for me.

Nancy sweeps in first, kissing both my cheeks. Cole Jr. and Wyatt orbit her legs until Wyatt stops dead and gawks. "Whoa. Are you a princess?"

I laugh, cheeks burning. "Not even close."

Someone kisses me on the cheek—Owen. Quick, warm, almost shy. My pulse goes haywire.

Julia presses baby Elise into my arms before I can protest, her voice calm, certain: "You'll be fine." And I am—somehow. Elise is lighter than air, her tiny hand curling around my thumb. For a moment everything else vanishes.

Speech (Jeff POV)

I can barely breathe watching Zoe cradle that baby. I never knew her weight at that age. Never held her. But tonight I see it, the echo. My daughter holding someone else's, steady hands despite the tremor. Julia takes Elise back, Theo brushing her temple with trembling fingers, and the circle loosens again.

***

At the dining table, I clear my throat, raise my glass.

"Before we eat—" My voice carries over the rooftop, soft but firm. "—I want to say something."

The chatter dies instantly. All eyes are on me. Carly stiff across the table, Bridget alert, Nancy already nodding. But only Zoe matters.

"This year," I say, "has been the most unexpected of my life. I thought my story was already written, every chapter finished. Turns out the best part hadn't even arrived yet."

Zoe stares, wide-eyed, breathless.

"I have a daughter," I continue. "Her name is Zoe MacKenzie. She was raised single-handedly by Carly." I nod towards Carly. "She is brave, stubborn, smart, hilarious—and she's teaching me every day what it means to be a father. She's the best thing that's ever happened to me. The best sentence I'll ever write."

I pause, because there's more. The words burn if I don't let them out.

"For years, I sent signals into the dark. Stories, fragments, characters—I didn't know if anyone was listening. I didn't even know who I was writing to. But she heard me. She found me. Zoe is my signal answered back."

The clink of glasses is still ringing when I lower mine. People are leaning in, buzzing, talking over each other — the tide of attention already spilling past me. Good. Let it go.

I glance across the table, and Carly's eyes catch mine.

She isn't smiling, not exactly. It's steadier than that. Something between appraisal and restraint, like she's weighing me in real time. For a second, it pins me harder than the toast itself.

Then, almost imperceptibly, she tips her head, drops her gaze, retreats back into her glass of water.

The applause, the chatter, the whole room keeps moving — but I'm still caught on that flicker of a look. It's not approval, not forgiveness, not anything I can name. Just a signal, small and devastating, that she heard me.

And for reasons I can't explain, that's enough to make my chest ache worse than any ovation ever could. It is more than nineteen years since our bodies were pressed together in that act that made Zoe and since that night I've told myself so many things. Mostly, I'm just devastated—by her pushing me away, her coldness, which I know is a mask for her fear of losing control, but it still hurts. Her never contacting me, never reaching out, never trying—that hurts too, but this I take partial responsibility for because it would have been so easy for me to do what she wouldn't do. All I can figure is that, during that long estrangement, I was afraid to overstep some invisible boundary.

I used to believe writing was shouting into a void. You made the trench coat darker, the rain louder, the femme fatale sharper, just to see if the echo would return. It never did.

So I kept writing, kept sending signals. A man chasing ghosts in alleys, a detective too angry to name his hunger. Every book was a flare fired into the night.

Then one day, a girl walked into my life and said her name was Zoe MacKenzie. My daughter. The signal I had been waiting for.

Comfortable (Zoe POV)

I don't care who sees. He said it. Out loud. With everyone listening. For once, I'm not invisible. For once, I'm in the center. My chest aches, but it's the best ache I've ever felt.

Blackthorn again. I'm now in Book 2: The Silent Widow. He spends half the book circling a woman who might save him or drown him—he can't decide. He never asks her what she wants. Typical.

And yet.

There's this one line where he almost admits he's lonely. Just one. Buried under all the cigarettes and blood. I swear it's Jeff talking straight to me, like he couldn't say it in real life so he made a detective say it in 1950 New Orleans.

It makes me want to throw the book across the room. Or hug it. Or both.

And when he raised that glass tonight, talking about signals and how he'd never miss mine—I wanted to believe him. I really did. But part of me wonders if he's been sending signals all along, through Blackthorn, and I was too late to catch them.

Olive Branch (Jeff POV)

As the clapping swells, I feel a tap at my arm. Carly. She tilts her head, eyes unreadable. "A word?"

I follow her down the stairs, away from the music and the hum. In the quiet loft below, she pulls a slim thumb drive from her bag and presses it into my palm.

"Pictures. Videos. Eighteen years," she says, voice clipped, businesslike. "The baby book, digitized. You should have it."

I stare at it. At her. "Carly, I—"

She presses the USB drive into my hand like it's nothing —like she's passing a library card. Her posture is stiff, her face arranged into neutrality, but I see the catch in her breath, the straightening of her shoulders before she lets go.

"Here," she says. "It's overdue. Just don't make me regret it."

Her tone is brisk, professional. Archivist, handing over metadata. But her fingers linger on the drive for a half-second longer than they need to. Skin to skin, the first touch in nineteen years, and something inside me cracks open, although it closes immediately, before I have a chance to know what it was.

That tiny pause lodges in me more than the words. It's not permission, not forgiveness, but it isn't dismissal either.

I pocket the drive and give a nod, like this is business. Like it doesn't feel like someone just cracked open the vault on nineteen years of silence.

She leaves before I can answer, heels sharp on the floor, moving back to the table and the party.

I look down at the drive, heavy in my hand. Years I missed. Years I'll never get back. But tonight, at least, she gave me this.

Chapter Thirty-One — Cake & Collision

Dinner/Cake (Zoe POV)

Plates are shifting, glasses clinking again, the hum of voices flooding back in after Dad's toast. I can still feel everyone's eyes on me, like they're waiting to see what I'll do with the weight he just set down. Dad comes back after Mom pulled him aside. I have no idea what that's about. I'm not sure I want to know.

Bridget leans over with that arched-eyebrow look of hers. "So, Zoe," she says, like it's a cross-examination, "have you decided on a major yet?"

I feel my face heat, but for once, I don't shrink from it. My fork is steady in my hand when I say, clear enough for the whole table to hear:

"Double major. English and Journalism, with a minor in History."

The word feels like a stone tossed into water, ripples spreading. I can see Dr. Lawson is pleased with my choice of minor.

Nancy raises her glass like she's sealing a verdict. "Words and truth. A Griffin combination if I've ever heard one."

I breathe out, slower now, letting it land. English with journalism. It sounds stitched together, messy maybe, but alive. Like Frankenstein's creation in the books I used to hide in. Like something I can make my own.

When I risk a glance to my right, Dad's already watching me. His smile is small, quiet, but it reaches his eyes. To my left, Mom is unreadable, but far from displeased. She seems thoughtful, mildly impressed, as if I've surprised her but not in a terrible way.

And for the first time tonight, I feel like I've chosen something that belongs to me.

***

The chatter has barely settled after my revelation when Nancy claps her hands like a stage manager. "Cake time!" she declares, and suddenly all eyes swing toward the table in the center of the roof.

The thing looks almost too pretty to touch — a piano-shaped cake, complete with white chocolate keys and black fondant sharps, buttercream roses curling along the edges. Gold piping glints in the string lights. I'm half afraid that if I cut into it, I'll ruin someone's art project.

Dad strikes a match and lights the candles — just two, a one recycled from Dad's cake in May, and a nine. The little flames flicker in the breeze, throwing tiny halos across the frosting.

Everyone sings "Happy Birthday" to my embarrassment and then —

"Make a wish," he says, and the way his eyes hold mine makes the noise of the roof fade.

I lean forward, cheeks hot, and blow them out. Everyone claps, off-key voices tumbling into a round of Happy Birthday that makes me laugh even though I want to hide my face.

The knife finds my hand — Nancy guiding, Bridget supervising, Carly watching like she's ready to criticize my slice ratio. The first cut squeaks through the fondant, and the whole roof cheers like I've just performed at Carnegie Hall.

I grin despite myself. For the first time all evening, I let the sweetness wash over me without fighting it.

***

After the cake and the clapping and the awful off-key chorus (Nancy swears she stayed in key; she did not), the gifts appear like a tide—bows, crisp bags, too much tissue paper rustling in the wind that skims the roof.

The generals go first. Bridget's is square and practical: a beautiful leather planner with tabs and a pen loop, monogrammed ZM. "Organization is freedom," she says, smiling too wide like it's a joke and also not a joke at all. I hug her; it smells like her office—paper and citrus hand cream.

Nancy's bag is tissue-armored. Inside: a silk scarf, deep cobalt with a subtle pattern that manages to whisper money without yelling it. "For when you want to look like you chose New York," she says, and kisses my cheek. I love it, even as my brain translates: elevate yourself.

Carly slides her gift across the table. The wrapping is neat, librarian precise. If it anyone else, I'd say the wrapping was professionally done, but this is my mom.

I peel it back and find a clothbound book, pale green with gold lettering on the spine: *Emma* by Jane Austen. Not a rare edition, or anything extravagant, but beautiful in its simplicity. A ribbon marker peeks out from the pages.

"I remember you saying it was your favorite Austen," Carly says, a little awkwardly, a little proud. "This edition caught my eye at the store. Thought you might like to have it for your shelf up here...in your other home." She glances at Jeff and then back at me.

My throat catches. *Emma*, the clever girl with too many schemes, with her indulgent father who loves her fiercely despite her missteps. I run my thumb over the gilt title, smiling faintly.

"Thanks, Mom," I say as I wrap her in a hug.

Carly smiles back, small but genuine, and for once it doesn't feel like a performance.

Theo presents a card from him and Julia—Elise's foot stamped in ink on the inside, the tiniest blue footprint in the world. I melt. The boys, Cole Jr. and Wyatt, have drawn me riding a motorcycle the size of a dinosaur. I melt again.

Then everything slows, like the air holds its breath, because Jeff stands and rakes a hand through his hair.

"Okay," he says, eyes on me. "Mine's...not really wrap-able."

A ripple of amusement passes through the group. He glances at Carly, at Bridget, at Nancy, then back to me. "You want to come downstairs for a minute?"

My heart thumps so hard I feel it in my throat. I nod.

He offers his hand. I take it.

We ride the elevator in a hush that feels enormous.

The garage opens up cool and echoing. He leads me past his bike toward the two spaces marked 5A. There's a shape under a dark cover. He stops. I look at him. He looks at me.

"Happy birthday, Zo," he says softly, and lifts the cover.

The silver Volvo shines like a secret pulled into daylight.

For a second I can't breathe. It's so solid, so safe. It's for me. My throat goes hot.

"XC40," he says, voice a little unsteady. "Fully electric, top safety ratings. Camera, sensors, the whole spaceship. Insurance handled, parking spot is ours. Lessons if you want them lined up—only if you want."

I press my fingers to my mouth. "Jeff…"

He pulls a small box from his pocket and opens it: the key fob, attached to a key chain with the Volvo logo. "You don't have to take it today," he adds quickly. "It can live here until you're ready. But it's yours."

I take the fob and then I'm hugging him, hard, before I realize I've moved. He holds on just as hard. For a beat the garage is only our breathing.

When we pull back, there's a sound behind us—heels on concrete. Carly and Bridget have appeared in the mouth of the aisle, Nancy half a step behind, arms folded.

Carly's mouth is a thin line. "Jeff."

"Carly," he says pleasantly, and then, to me, like we're the only two people in the room again: "You deserve to move through the world without asking permission."

I nod, blinking. I do not cry. (I almost cry.)

Bridget takes in the car, then me, then Jeff. She exhales. "Well," she says, a compromise between admiration and dismay. "At least it's not a motorcycle."

"Working on that," Jeff mutters.

"Over my dead body," Carly says, but there's no real venom; there's a look I can't read, old and tired, and something else, newer.

Nancy just lifts her chin. "Good choice," she tells Jeff, like she's grading a paper and he finally wrote the thesis.

We go back up together, the elevator a little crowded. I still have the fob in my palm. My hand won't unclench.

Back on the roof, the wind has picked up, carrying the smell of frosting and city. Everyone looks at me like I've stepped through a door and closed it behind me.

I kind of have.

Awkward (Jeff POV)

For a second in that garage, when Zoe's arms lock around me, I think: This is the whole book. This right here. Then the chorus arrives and the spell loosens. I keep my voice even; I do not rise to Carly's bait; I let Nancy grade me. I can handle adult politics if I get to see my kid glow like that.

Theo signs a deadpan, [nice spaceship] and Julia grins before returning her happy expression to baby Elise in her arms. My nephews demand if they can honk the horn (no).

It's a challenge getting back on the elevator. We have to split up. Cole and my nephews, Ed, Ethan, Augie and Dr. Lawson head up first. I hover behind the rest and wait for each person to get on the next ride up—Owen and Zoe, now clutching the fob, Nancy and Bridget. I say, "After you," to Carly, but for some reason I take a step too soon and collide into her sideways. I'm hit with a wave of jasmine and vanilla, mixed with the wine on her breath. I blink. She laughs and stutters an apology. Nancy finds our embarrassment amusing. "Get a room," she says. When I recover my senses, I glare at her.

As soon as the doors open again, I gesture for Carly to go before me. I block the door with my hand, waiting for the other ladies to walk past. As I fall into step with Nancy, she shoots me a look. "What the hell was that, Jeff? You're not falling for Carly, are you?"

"What?" I ask, more high-pitched than I intend.

"You could cut the tension between you two with a knife. It's none of my business, but, Jeff, are you sure you want to make that mistake again?"

She walks on, leaving me to contemplate her words. Christ. I've made a lot of mistakes in my life, but Carly is not the one I regret. All I have to do is think of Zoe, the consequence I don't deserve, and I'm done. But as for repeating the Carly mistake, it's impossible. There's too much water under the bridge. She concealed Zoe from me for eighteen years and, when I confronted her, when I told her in no uncertain terms that I was going to be Zoe's father now that I knew, she was openly hostile to me. This is not a woman I'm in danger of falling for again.

Back on the roof, the presents drift back to simple. Augie gives Zoe a tiny tin of espresso caramels with a handwritten "open when the world is loud." Dr. Lawson lifts her paper cup and declares, "Independence is the only sensible gift," and then adds, "that and a seatbelt," which, fair. (She winks at my kid as she hands her a gift bag, out of which Zoe pulls a brand new hardcover biography of Eleanor Roosevelt.)

I feel lighter than I have in years.

Then Owen Aubrey clears his throat.

He's been good tonight—discreet, never crowding. He steps forward now, careful with the air.

"Zoe," he says, accent softening my daughter's name into something that sounds like music. He holds out a flat, wrapped rectangle and a folded page tucked under twine. "Two small things. One borrowed from the past, one from…now."

She unwraps the book first: Franny and Zooey, a worn older edition that looks like it has belonged to someone's heart. Inside the cover, an inscription in pencil:

> For Z.M.—
>
> You make the quiet feel like the point.
>
> —O.A.

She presses her thumb to the margin like she's steadying herself. Then she takes the folded page and opens it. It's a poem—his—and he doesn't read it out loud, thank God, but the room contracts anyway, like everyone feels the tender.

I have the immediate, ridiculous impulse to stand between them.

I don't.

She looks up at him, a little stunned. "Thank you," she says, blushing pink.

I watch Owen fumble through his words, trying to play it cool and failing in the most obvious way. Zoe's eyes light up anyway. She doesn't see the stiffness, the overthought phrasing, the awkwardness of it all — she sees the sincerity underneath.

She tucks the poem inside the book and then slips away toward the balcony. Owen hesitates, glances at me—good—and then follows her, quieter than a shadow.

And suddenly, I'm floored. Because I've seen this dance before.

Carly, all those years ago, trying too hard to seem composed. Formal when she should've been natural. Correcting me when she should've just laughed.

Her laugh. Honestly. It's Carly's laugh that stays with me more than anything. But she always had one layer of armor too many, and yet beneath it, a fire she never let burn where anyone could see.

Owen's not Carly. Not exactly. But the parallel is close enough that it twists something inside me.

Because if Zoe can find patience for that kind of fumbling sincerity, if she can look past the stiffness to the heart, then maybe—God help me—so can I.

What am I saying? Carly and I are not going to happen. Carly and I cannot happen.

Nancy's hand is suddenly on my sleeve, stopping me from following Zoe to the elevator. "Stay," she murmurs. I sit and helplessly watch Owen follow her instead.

Carly is watching, too. For once, we're the same animal: two people terrified of the same thing for different reasons, perhaps.

I make myself breathe.

Let her have air.

Let her choose.

Chapter Thirty-Two — Signals in the Night

Owen's Explanation (Zoe POV)

The band is playing "3AM" as the party hums around me.
The chatter, the clinking glasses, the warm summer air—
all of it feels too big, too loud. I slip away toward the door
that opens into the loft, clutching Owen's book and poem.
My heart pounds as I make my way down the stairs,
down the ladder from the mezzanine, and then step
outside again, the city glittering below, a reef of lights.

Owen follows, sliding the door of the balcony closed
behind him. He doesn't touch me. Just stands beside me,
hands shoved in his pockets, eyes on the street like it has
the answers.

"I'm sorry I've been… rubbish," he says finally, his accent
softening the word. "I didn't want to bulldoze your life.
Figured you've got enough waves right now."

"Understatement," I mutter, but it makes me smile.

Silence settles between us, warm, loaded. He glances at
me, nervous but brave. "Zoe—would it be alright if I
kissed you again?"

My body answers before my mouth does. "Yes."

He leans in slowly, asking once more with his eyes, and when his lips brush mine, it's unhurried and careful. But it sparks anyway, rearranging the air. My second kiss, but somehow it feels like the first real one. The one that matters.

When we part, I'm grinning like an idiot. He is too. "Happy birthday," he whispers.

"Yeah," I breathe. "It is."

Above, I glimpse my father at the railing on the roof, watching. I lift the book slightly as if to say: See? I'm okay. He nods once, shaky but proud. For the first time all night, the static eases. The signal comes through, clear.

Letting Go (Jeff POV)

From the railing above, I watch my daughter kiss a boy for the first time that I can clearly see. My chest tightens like it's being pulled in two directions. Pride and panic, both tearing at me. She looks older suddenly—not the girl who stumbled into my loft a few months ago, but a young woman stepping into her own.

I grip the railing until my knuckles ache. Instinct says 'shield her,' but another part of me whispers: *this is what safe looks like too. A boy who asks. A boy who sees her.*

I force myself to breathe. To let her have this.

That's when Carly steps up beside me. Too close. The wine has loosened her, a faint giggle in her throat, her shoulder brushing mine as she leans in to look. The city hums, and the band below shifts to "Photograph."

For a breath, the air between us charges. My pulse stutters at the tilt of her head, the nearness, the possibility. Almost.

I tear my eyes away, grounding myself on Zoe's glow. No. Not Carly. Not again.

She exhales beside me, her voice softer than usual. "Don't let her pay for your mistakes."

I don't answer. I can't. The distance between us is the only thing keeping me steady.

Carly's Gifts (Zoe POV)

Before I can rejoin the party on the roof, Carly pulls me aside. Owen returns without me, back up through the loft and the private door to the roof that we haven't used much tonight, while Carly and I settle on the couch. Her voice is low and soft.

"You've done the work," she says, eyes flicking over me. "Therapy. School. Keeping yourself together. I see that, Zoe. And I'm proud."

The word proud stuns me, lodging in my chest.

She opens her bag and pulls out a velvet box first. Inside, a delicate necklace glints in the string lights. She removes the necklace from the little box and holds it up. "Your grandparents wanted to be here, but as you know, they're just not up for the trip. Your grandmother wore this when she was your age. She wanted you to have it."

She moves closer and fastens the necklace around my neck. I finger the aquamarine pendant gratefully. "Thanks, Mom."

"It was a gift from your great-grandparents. Aquamarine is your grandmother's birthstone."

Then she hands me a small brass case, also retrieved from her purse. Inside: two smooth, polished stress balls, weighty in my palm. "From your grandfather. He thought you'd understand why."

I do. My grandfather, the elder MacKenzie, battled anxiety and a relentless urge to fidget his entire life.

Finally, she slides out a tissue-wrapped frame. I unwrap it and find a photograph: Carly, Bridget, and Jeff in their college days, grinning on some battered couch, the three of them alive with a moment long gone.

"Before everything," she murmurs. "I wanted you to see it. To know it existed."

My throat catches. "Thank you, Mom."

She nods once. No lecture, no edge. Just that.

Our Dance (Jeff POV)

The band segues into Dylan's "Forever Young," the chords floating out under the string lights. Zoe finds me in the crowd. I can see the question in her eyes before she even moves.

I offer my hand. She takes it.

The chatter fades as we step into the open space together. A father and daughter dance—just ours. Everyone watches, but it feels like no one else is here.

Her hand rests light in mine. She's 19, radiant, alive, yet still my kid. I guide her slowly, careful not to step on her toes, the song's lyrics ghosting through the night like a benediction.

May you stay... forever young.

Her head tilts against my chest for a moment, and my throat burns. Around us, the rooftop blurs—the lights, the city, even the guests. All I see is her.

Then, across the space, I feel another signal. Carly. She's off to the side, arms folded, her expression carefully neutral. But her eyes hold. They stay with me longer than they should, longer than anyone else's.

For a flicker, it's not the music or Zoe's small hand in mine that steadies me—it's that look. The echo of a laugh I can't forget, carried now in Zoe's smile, colliding with her mother's gaze across the rooftop.

Carly blinks, the mask sliding back into place, and I'm left wondering if I imagined the whole thing.

...but it's Zoe, and me, just the two of us now, circling under the stars. For the first time in years, I don't feel haunted by what I missed. I feel anchored by what I have.

And I swear, I'll never let the signal break again.

Musing Later (Zoe POV)

From the Journal of Zoe Griffin MacKenzie:

The song was ours. At least, it was supposed to be. Dad and me, spinning clumsily under the string lights while the Echo Union singer tried to capture the Dylan essence...a tall order, but none of that mattered. All I heard, really, was the melody. And all I felt was, him, and me.

Until, suddenly, I saw it. The shift in his eyes. One second locked on me, the next flicking past my shoulder, pinning to her. Mom.

It wasn't long, not even a heartbeat, but it was real. A signal, tiny but undeniable.

And I don't know how to feel about it.

Part of me—maybe the biggest part—wants them to be happy. Isn't that what kids are supposed to wish for? Parents finding their way back to each other? It would stitch the whole story together in a way that feels neat, clean, hopeful.

But another part of me, the selfish part I don't want to admit, bristled. I just got him. Finally. And already, another signal's pulling him away, even if it's her. Even if it's always been her.

I don't know what it means yet. Maybe nothing. Maybe everything.

All I know is, for those three minutes, I felt like the center of his world. And I'm not ready to let that go.

Chapter Thirty-Three — After the Party

Clearest Signal (Jeff POV)

The party thins the way a tide pulls back—plates stacked, the last tealights guttering in jars, string lights humming over a breeze that smells like pastry sugar and summer stone. I'm collecting forks into a towel when Bridget appears, arms folded, mouth already slanting toward a smirk.

"Congratulations, Griffin," she says. "On turning a year older and into a better man."

"Better man is doing a lot of work there," I tell her.

She tilts her head. "I've seen you try to get away with charm before. Tonight wasn't that." Her eyes flick toward the roof's edge where the little balcony hangs over the street. "You put her at the center. That speech? Risky for a girl who doesn't love the spotlight. But it was honest."

I shrug because I don't know where to put the warmth that crawls up my neck. "She's...worth being honest for."

"Try 'non-negotiable,'" Bridget says, softer now. A beat. "Fatherhood looks good on you."

"Better than boyfriend did," I say lightly.

She huffs a laugh. "You were catastrophically bad at that."

We let it sit. The city hums below us, unbothered.

Her voice drops. "Don't screw this up, Jeff. She trusts you. That's a rare weather pattern. Protect it." She squeezes my arm once—a benediction disguised as a warning—and peels away to collect Edward and Ethan, who are angling for one last slice of piano-key cake.

I'm still standing there with the towel when Nancy steps in, all crossed arms and audit gaze. She's cataloging: the tables, the trash bags tied neatly, the clean knife, my face.

"Well?" I say, because if I don't break the ice she'll freeze me into it.

She doesn't smile, not at first. "She's lovely," Nancy says. "Skittish around the edges, but lovely." A slow nod, like she's stamping a document. "Worthy to be a Griffin."

The air leaves my lungs in a way that embarrasses me. I cover it with a swallow. "Thank you."

Nancy smiles now. "You did better tonight than I expected."

"High praise."

"Don't ruin it by keeping her in the dark." Her eyes catch mine, level and unsparing. "You hide because you're afraid. I get it. But secrecy is a kind of cruelty, even when you mean it as love."

There it is—the line I deserve. I nod. "I hear you."

She studies me a heartbeat longer, then reaches out and straightens a skew string light as if that might straighten me, too. "Good night, little brother." She kisses my cheek —quick, almost furtive—and heads toward the door, calling the boys in her no-nonsense voice.

I stand alone with the faint sugar of the cake and the sound of the city and try to name the feeling that sits under my ribs: terror, yes, but braided with something steady. Not triumph. Not yet. Just the strange relief of being seen—and still chosen…still caught in the signal.

Catching the Signal (Zoe POV)

Up in my nook, I peel the pins from my hair and let them clink into the bowl I pretend is for jewelry. The night hangs blurry at the edges—candles, clapping, the careful way Jeff looked at me when he said the word daughter into a microphone like it had a heat that might burn if he didn't hold it right.

I lie back and stare at the ceiling. My lips still feel electric.

Owen's hand at my cheek. *May I?* The question, soft and old-fashioned and exactly right. The way the city air touched my shoulders on the balcony and the whole world went quiet except for my heart doing its dumb drum thing. The kiss itself—gentle, certain. My first real one. The kind that doesn't erase you, but underlines you.

For a second, panic tries the door. Did Jeff see? What will he think? The old loop revs, but I catch it this time, like Julia taught me. In—four. Hold—four. Out—six. "You're here," I tell myself. "You're safe." The door in my head closes softly.

I flip to my side and think about the other part of the night: Aunt Nancy watching me like a hawk who's trying to decide if I'm prey or family; Bridget doing that cool thing she does where she smiles with only her eyes; Carly pretending not to be counting how many bites of cake I took. The generals. I can feel them measuring me, measuring us. It makes me want to stand taller and crawl under a table at the same time.

Were they impressed? Did I pass? Will I always be auditioning to belong?

Maybe. Maybe that's life. Maybe the point isn't the audition. Maybe the point is that I got to stand under a sky of café lights with people who, for all their edges, came because of me. Because of us.

I touch my mouth and feel the ghost of a smile. Tonight was messy—there's the present I didn't open yet (while we danced, Jeff said he has one more to give, later) and the weird ache I get when Jeff folds into himself and thinks I don't notice, and Owen's poem that I'm going to reread until the words wear thin—but something true cut through the static.

The signal was clear, just for a while.

I close my eyes and breathe like I learned, counting long enough for the city to settle. Through the skylight, I think I hear his step on the roof stairs, slow and thoughtful. I don't know what comes next. Not exactly. But for the first time in a long time, the not-knowing feels like possibility instead of threat.

It feels—maybe—like ours.

Epilogue

One More Present (Zoe POV)

I sit on the edge of my bed, smoothing the quilt, curious.

He doesn't sit. He paces once, twice, then places a manila envelope on my desk. His hand lingers too long, as if he's debating taking it back.

"What's that?" I ask.

He exhales. "Something I never thought I'd share."

Cautiously, I slip the envelope open. Inside is a stack of pages, a title page on top. Fragments.

No subtitle. No dedication. Just the word.

My throat tightens. "You finished it?"

"Not finished," he says quickly, his voice rough. "It's a draft. Messy. Ugly in places. I nearly talked myself out of it a hundred times." He swallows. "But you...you deserve to know me. The whole of me. Not just the scraps I let slip."

I hug the stack to my chest, not ready to turn a page. "This is...your gift to me?"

His nod is sharp, betraying the fear beneath — the raw terror of being seen. "You gave me a gift I'll never forget, Zo. That melody...your grandfather's hands through yours. This—" he gestures toward the manuscript—"is mine to you. No performance. No audience. Just us."

Before he can retreat into himself, I throw my arms around him, the manuscript pressed between us. "Thank you," I whisper. "Thank you for trusting me."

He holds me tight. It feels like breathing after drowning.

When he eases back, he gestures to my lamp. "Don't stay up too late." It's half a joke, half a plea.

"Good night, Dad," I whisper, and the word hangs like a blessing.

By the time he reaches the bottom of the ladder, I'm already cross-legged on the bed, the manuscript in my lap. As if I've been waiting my whole life for this.

***

The lamplight bends shadows across the pages. My hands tremble as I begin.

> *I cheated. That's what prompted the fight with Bridget. I told myself it wasn't cheating, that it didn't mean anything, but of course it did. Bridget found out; she always found out. It wasn't the cheat itself that broke us, but the lie. The way I*

swore it was nothing when she knew it was everything. She didn't cry, she didn't scream. She just walked, and I let her go.

My stomach twists. Bridget—my aunt, my godmother. My mom's best friend. I press the page to my chest and force myself to keep reading.

> *The night with Carly wasn't romance. It wasn't even desire, not really. It was liquor, loneliness, and the pathetic comfort of proximity. One night. I told myself it meant nothing, so I could pretend it hadn't happened. But life takes what you pretend doesn't matter and shoves it down your throat later. Out of that nothing came everything—Zoe.*

My name in his voice on the page makes me go still. The room spins. I've never thought I'd see it written down, ugly and undeniable. And yet, here it is.

I turn the page.

> *In the years after, I didn't have relationships. I had distractions. Women who didn't want much from me, because I didn't want to give much back. Some were beautiful, some brilliant, some bored housewives who thought sleeping with a writer made them dangerous. I never wanted any of them to stay. If they stayed, they'd see the hollow place inside me. So I made sure they didn't. I told myself it was freedom, but it was just cowardice dressed up as independence.*

I set the stack down, cover my face with both hands. He's giving me everything—the rawest pieces, the parts he never showed anyone.

When I pick the pages up again, my hands are steadier.

***

The words blur until I find it.

> *And then there was you.*
>
> *Not because of me. Because of Carly, because of timing, because of the bottle I never should've touched. You were the consequence I didn't deserve. The miracle I didn't expect.*
>
> *You are the part of my life I'll never call a mistake. The sentence that makes sense of every fragment. The one thing I would write a thousand times over, even knowing all the pain between then and now.*

My hand flies to my mouth. I read it again. And again. The words don't erase the ugly. They don't have to. They steady me.

For the first time I see it clearly: the fragments aren't just about failure. They're about survival — about finding me on the other side of everything he thought had ruined him.

I close the pages and press them to my chest.

I flip through the pages, my breath catching. It's all here. Every fragment, every ghost of a sentence he never said out loud.

Instead of breaking me, it makes me feel more whole than I've ever been.

There is one more fragment that gives me pause. I turn another page and find it, tucked between denser paragraphs, and I notice the ink on the page is fresh, as if he just typed it out tonight:

> *Sometimes I think life is just shadows across a wall. A man chasing silhouettes, too far away to catch, too close to ignore. I've spent years trying to name them, to hold them still. And then one day, one of them turned, and she wasn't a shadow at all. She was my daughter. My signal. The one thing real enough to stop the chase.*

I read it twice, my throat tight. He doesn't say "Harley" or whatever femme fatale might've haunted his notebooks. Because, yes, I know that when he talks about "chasing silhouettes," it's Blackthorn chasing the femme fatale. That's Jeff, hiding in plain sight (for me anyway) behind his protagonist.

But here he says it's me that made him stop the chase.

And for now, that's enough.

***

Across the loft, I see him at his desk in the pool of light, the glow of his MacBook painting pale shadows on his face. Videos play—Carly's, the years I thought were lost: me in a tutu, wobbling through a recital; me at seven, blowing out birthday candles; me in glasses too big for my face.

For a moment we're two halves of the same scene: me reading him into being, him watching me grow in fast-forward.

I press my palm to the page. He lifts his hand to the screen. The connection hums.

"Dad," I whisper across the silence though he can't hear me. "We're both catching up, aren't we?"

Dawn (Jeff POV)

I don't sleep. Every sound from above stirs me—my imagination painting her bent over the pages, eyes moving across the words I never thought I'd let anyone see.

There are fragments I did not give her. Not yet. My secret file. I wrote another one of those tonight.

> *The truth is, the silhouettes were never strangers. They were her. Always her. The woman I couldn't stop wanting, couldn't stop losing. Carly. Every Blackthorn femme fatale was just another way of drawing her back into the room. And I never stopped chasing the shadow she left behind.*

This is something that was difficult enough to admit to myself, let alone share with our daughter. Maybe it's not even true. Maybe it's just the excitement of the night, blurring my senses. It struck me hard because the feeling goes along with another fragment in my Secret File, something I wrote about my character Harley:

Harley didn't walk onto the page fully formed. She leaked out of me. Drop by drop, from every silence I swallowed.

The first draft, she wasn't even a woman. Just a shadow in a bar mirror, all teeth and laughter. But the shadow kept coming back, demanding flesh. Demanding a name.

Harley. I don't know where I stole it from. A motorcycle ad in a magazine? The sound of it— hard at the start, all heat in the middle, soft at the end. A name that burns but still rolls off the tongue like smoke.

She was supposed to be a distraction. A trick of the genre. A foil for Blackthorn, someone to keep him sharp. But then I gave her too much. Her stride, her laugh, the way she tilted her chin when she knew she'd won. None of it was invented. It was memory, dressed up as fiction. Memory I'd buried, suddenly clawing out of the dirt.

Readers thought Harley was clever writing. A trope bent into something dangerous and sexy. But I knew. She wasn't clever writing. She was a ghost I couldn't exorcise.

People ask me where my characters come from. I say the usual things—books I've read, films I loved, late nights in New Orleans bars. I never say: she came from one night I couldn't forget, from a woman who haunted me long before she ever left me.

I never say: Harley was never just Harley.

I don't know if Harley somehow emerged gradually from the shadows of my subconscious, echoes of Carly. Whatever the case, these two fragments are now tucked safely in my secret file, locked away in the safe.

By the time dawn bleeds pale light into the loft, I'm already in the kitchen, trying to look busy with coffee and eggs, my hands unsteady. The city outside is muted, still rubbing its eyes awake.

The ladder creaks. I look up. She comes down, hair mussed, manuscript hugged to her chest like she carried it all night. Her eyes are puffy—not just from lack of sleep, but tears.

My chest tightens. I wipe my palms on a dish towel, bracing.

She sets the pages carefully on the counter, like they're sacred. Then she looks at me—really looks—and her voice is soft, trembling.

"I stayed up all night. I couldn't stop."

My throat works. "That bad, huh?"

She shakes her head, fierce. "That real. Dad, I feel like I finally met you. Not the you from Wikipedia, or the writer, or the guy with the loft. You."

I grip the counter edge, trying to steady myself. "And?"

When she steps closer, brushing my arm, she adds: "And…I'm proud. I don't care what the world thinks of the ugly parts. They don't scare me. What scares me is you shutting me out of them."

My throat closes, the sting in my eyes sharp and unrelenting. I pull her into my arms, coffee forgotten, eggs burning faintly in the pan.

She buries her face in my chest. "Thank you for letting me in."

I press my chin to the crown of her head. "Thank you for staying."

The kitchen light glows against the rising sun, and for a long moment, the morning feels like the cleanest page I've ever been given.

Eating breakfast (Zoe POV)

The manuscript sits between us on the counter. My hands linger on the pages, sensing the aliveness of the passages. Of him. Jeffrey William Griffin, my dad, fragments forming the whole. "I couldn't stop," I whisper. "It's you. All of you."

He looks up from his plate. Having ruined the eggs, we're eating waffles. So much more fitting. Waffles are for us.

"Reading it," I go on, "I'm more certain than ever."

His brows knit. "Of what?" I can see the fear in his eyes. Will it ever go away, his fear of rejection?

"My major," I say softly. "English and Journalism. History on the side. It felt impossible before. But after last night, connecting with you, the truth, all of it, even the ugly parts, I knew that words are where I belong."

Belonging (Jeff POV)

I can't speak right away. I feel winded by the tidal wave of emotions sweeping through me. She still hasn't run. She's here, not out of pity but love. Something else too. Awe.

I think about LSU, where I shuffled between majors like cards I couldn't hold. History, Drama, French, French literature, Literature. By the summer session between second and third years, I'd settled on Creative Writing. It felt less like a choice and more like…a sentence. A life sentence, I suppose. For her, it sounds like freedom.

Now she's telling me that…what is she telling me? That the ugliest parts of my soul have convinced her that these words—no, words, just words, she said—and yet *these* words did the talking. *My* words spelled out the truth of where she belongs. She seems to be telling me that she's proud to be part of me, that these words, being my story, somehow give her the resolution to start forming her own.

"I'm proud of you, Zo." The words are heavy, weighed down by envy, relief, wonder. Fear. Yes, fear, because she's not just my daughter anymore. She's about to become my peer.

She gives me a side hug. I kiss her on the top of her head. For a moment, over waffles and wreckage, I dare to believe that she is proud to belong to me.

Signal Across Time (Zoe POV)

By afternoon, the rooftop party feels like another world, a distant memory, the glasses stacked, the laughter of last night already folded into memory. Downstairs, the loft feels like another world—still, waiting. The piano lamp glows like a lighthouse.

"I have something for you," I whisper. "Just you."

My hands tremble as I play. Not Beethoven, not Schubert, but the jazz line I found tucked in his father's songbook, marked up with edits, heavy with history.

The notes weave into the loft—fragile, alive, not perfect but ours.

When the last chord fades, I don't look up. Finally, I risk it. He's standing still, eyes wet.

"Zo..." His voice frays. "That was my father's."

"I know," I whisper. "I thought maybe... it could be yours too."

He crushes me into his chest. His breath shudders against my hair.

Genesis (Jeff POV)

My father's hands were never gentle. They were calloused from work, rough from years of gripping tools and typewriter keys. A lawyer by profession, but endless other things: stamp collector, old chevy mechanic, antique restorer. When he pulled the harmonica out of his pocket, or touched a piano, the touch was soft. I never understood how one man could hold so much contradiction—hard and tender, brutal and graceful. But then, years later, I hear the melody in Zoe's fingers. It's like hearing him again, only better. Her light. Her innocence.

Her arms are still around me, the faint echo of the melody vibrating in my chest long after the piano fell silent.

Not yet, I think. Not all the darkness yet. Tonight is hers.

I close my eyes, press my chin to her head. "Zo," I manage. "That was… everything."

She looks up, tears mirrored in both our eyes.

And for the first time in my life, I believe it—the story isn't ending.

It's beginning again.

THE END

www.ingramcontent.com/pod-product-compliance
Lightning Source LLC
Chambersburg PA
CBHW021408110726
47901CB00008B/2104